VERY LONG ODDS, AT BEST
Gambling With The IRS

Don Dignam

authorHOUSE®

AuthorHouse™
1663 Liberty Drive
Bloomington, IN 47403
www.authorhouse.com
Phone: 1-800-839-8640

Published by AuthorHouse   07/18/2012

ISBN: 978-1-4772-3672-7 (sc)
ISBN: 978-1-4772-3671-0 (e)

Library of Congress Control Number: 2012911850

VERY LONG ODDS, AT BEST

u

At 4:30 on Friday afternoon Tony walked out of the Oakwood Inn and headed toward his car. This stop had been the last of his business calls for the day and he was looking forward to getting home and relaxing for the weekend.

Just as he was about to hit his remote to unlock the car door he was approached by two men, one in shirt sleeves, as one would expect on a hot summer afternoon, and another wearing a buttoned suit coat.

"Hey Tony, we would like to talk to you for a minute," the one not wearing a coat called.

Tony stopped dead in his tracks and turned to face the two strangers. "Talk about what, and who the hell are you?"

The two men came nearer to Tony, and the one closest to him flashed a badge of some sort and responded, "We're agents with the Internal Revenue Service and we would like to talk to you about your income tax returns."

"Talk to me about tax returns? Here in the middle of the street? Come on, cut the bullshit, my boss sent you didn't he?" Tony said in a half-joking voice.

The stranger in the suit coat offered, "It's no bullshit Tony. We think you might have some explaining to do."

"I'm still not buying it," came Tony's rejoinder. He went on, "I know the IRS guys are supposed to be tough, but this is nuts, if it's true. Why here in the middle of the street, and why at this time of the day?"

"Well Mr. D'Angelo" began one of the agents, "you're a bit difficult to catch up with. Seems you are rarely home, and when you are at work you're all over the place, so here's as good a place as any."

"I like moving around. It's harder to hit a moving target and maybe this is a good time and place for you, buddy, but not for me. If you want to talk to me about taxes you are going to have to talk to my lawyer first."

Tony began to reach toward the back pocket of the slacks he was wearing when all of a sudden the agent wearing the suit coat quickly reached his right hand into his jacket and shouted, "Hold it Tony, what are you doing?"

"I'm getting my wallet so I can give you my attorney's business card. Is that okay?"

"That won't be necessary, we know who he is and where we can reach him. Just bring your hand back around where I can see it. Do you want to call the mouth piece, or should we do that?"

With clear irritation in his voice Tony said, "You call him, I don't have time for this crap."

The conversation ended with one of the agents telling Tony that if things went the way the IRS expected things to go, Tony may well have plenty of free time on his hands in the not too distant future, followed by, "have a nice weekend, Tony."

With that parting shot ringing in his ears, Tony got into his Lexus and began negotiating his way through the evening's rush-hour traffic. All the way home, of course, the conversation with the agents and the possible repercussions raced through his mind. "What was the trigger that set this off?" "Did someone blow the whistle?" 'Maybe it's just a fishing expedition?" "If they really had something they would want to do more than just talk, wouldn't they?"

Questions continued to race through his mind as Tony drove into the driveway of his home. Unfortunately, no answers became apparent to him.

u

I t was just after six in the evening when Tony turned the knob on the front door. The door swung open without his having to turn his key in the lock, again. "Damn it," he said to himself. He had harped on his son and daughter over and over again about keeping the door to their suburban house locked, even when they were home, and especially when they were home alone.

Tony closed the door behind him and locked it with the double bolt. As he laid his keys on the credenza in the foyer he listened but heard no sounds emanating from any other part of the house. "Well, guess it's going to be a late supper again" he thought. After hanging his suit coat over the back of a chair in the dining room he headed off to the family room. As he moved in that direction he consoled himself by saying, "I guess I'll just have a few cherries to appease my hunger pangs until dinner is ready." Of course the cherries would be the garnish in his favorite drink, the Rob Roy.

As Tony entered the family room he for the first time since entering the house heard the voice of another person, his teenaged daughter Angela. The girl was lying on the sofa in front of the fireplace with her cell phone glued to the side of her head. Angela gave her father the courtesy of waving to him to acknowledge the fact that she recognized him.

Had this occurred at the local shopping mall no such acknowledgement would have taken place. Teenagers generally prefer to disassociate themselves from parents when in the presence of their peers. On the other hand, just because another person was present there was no need to discontinue the "urgent" conversation in which Angela was currently involved.

Tony gave a wave back to his daughter, and then proceeded to the small cocktail bar in the corner of the room. Although small in physical appearance, the bar had all the amenities one might desire in a home-based watering hole.

This nightly ritual began with extracting a double-size cocktail glass from under the bar. Next the glass was filled with cubes from the under-bar refrigerator, and the glass was placed upon the rubber drink-mixing pad atop the bar. Then the 1.75 ML bottle of Dewars scotch was uncapped and a generous portion of the amber liquid was dispensed into the glass, filling it to within just a fraction of the way to its lip. No device, such as a shot glass, was used to measure the volume of liquid being poured into the glass. Experience had endowed Tony with the knowledge of just how much was enough. Next came a minimal splash of sweet vermouth, just enough to lightly deaden the harshness experienced by drinking straight Scotch whisky.

The deed had been done, except for the final flourish, the crowning glory. A large container of Maraschino Cherries was uncapped, and with great aplomb, three of its contents were dropped into the glass holding the core elements of Tony's drink. Now Tony was ready to get serious about learning the whereabouts of his spouse, Laura, and his son Nicholas.

"Hey Angie, it's me your father," Tony announced to his daughter. "How about ungluing that phone from your head so I can ask you a question?"

With a quick and exasperated "Gotta go now" the teenager put the telephone aside. "Hi dad" she said, and then came to a sitting position on the sofa upon which she had been sprawled while no doubt discussing the major crises in the world, most of which emanated from the high school where she was currently in her sophomore year.

"Hi yourself, where's the rest of the clan?"

To which he received an "I dunno" from his daughter.

"Excuse me" said Tony, followed by "What's an I dunno?"

"Why are you asking me such a silly question?" was the best he could coax out of his daughter.

"Angela," he began with some sternness in his voice, "I speak the English language rather well, and I am a college graduate, but I must admit that I am somewhat deficient in foreign languages. The term "I dunno" doesn't ring a bell with me. Did you perchance intend to answer my question by saying "I don't know?"

"Of course" Angela replied by following with, "I said," but Tony jumped in. "Don't say it again!"

Tony began to rant. "What the hell is this world coming to? I went way in over my head to buy this house in this community because the schools here are supposed to be first class. This is America, and from that I assume the schools will teach students to speak the English language. But what do I hear coming from the mouths of my children? How about I dunno, I gotta, I seen him, and God only knows what else."

"Any way, may I have an answer to my question that I can understand?"

"Sorry Dad," Angela began. "I just got home a few minutes ago from volleyball practice. I haven't seen mom or Nicky since I left for school this morning."

"I'm sorry too," said Tony. "I didn't mean to yell, but I just had a rather upsetting experience and I was hoping to find your mother home so I could discuss it with her," Tony said in a soft voice.

"Well, Dad, you can talk to me."

"Thanks, sweetheart, but I'm afraid this is an adult subject, and as smart as you are, I don't think you would be able to provide answers to the questions I plan to ask your mother. I'm not even sure your mother will have the answers," came Tony's reply, followed by his taking a long swig on the drink he had prepared earlier.

"I don't get it." Tony thought to himself as he moved toward his favorite chair and seated himself in front of the television set. "Laura, my wife of 20 years, doesn't work, thanks to my busting my ass bringing home the bacon, so why is it she isn't home most of the time when I get home from work?"

"It's a good thing I have the right genes and that the kids are active in school activities or we would all be part of the fat-people problem in this country. I think the next time I have a poker night I'll invite the Colonel, Ronald McDonald and the guy who founded Wendy's. Maybe I can get some of my money back."

Just as he was about to hit the remote control and turn on the television he heard the door leading from the garage to the kitchen close. Seconds later Laura walked into the room and announced that supper was on the counter in the kitchen.

"Wow, you must be the fastest cook in the world," was Tony's greeting.

"Very funny. I see your tough work schedule hasn't dulled your sense of humor, or should I say sarcasm skills?"

"Look" she went on, "with all the goofy schedules the four of us keep, how the hell am I supposed to maintain any kind of a meal schedule? And even if I did cook elaborate meals, what are the odds that all four of us would sit down at the table together? I do the best that I can, and if that isn't good enough maybe you need to hire a cook?"

After listening again to the now all to often repeated conversation between her parents, Angela excused herself and headed toward the kitchen.

Tony went on, "Hire a cook, what a brilliant idea. And while we are at it, let's get a laundress and a housekeeper."

"Don't forget a chauffer to drive the kids around to all of their social and school functions."

Laura noticed the cocktail glass on the table next to where Tony was sitting and said, "I see you have begun to prime the pump again."

"In case you haven't figured it out yet, I need something around here to help me maintain my sanity," he shot back.

"I suggest you up the dosage because what you have been doing doesn't seem to be working very well."

"Look, Laura, let's cut the bullshit. I need to discuss something serious with you, so can we dispense with all of the usual crap?"

"In awhile. I want to watch something on the TV right now. Where's the remote?" is all he heard in response to an attempt to bring some sanity to their conversation.

With that Tony got up from his chair and headed off to the kitchen. On the way out of the room he flipped the remote control to Laura, and said, "Here, with any luck at all this thing will backfire and fry your ass."

u

With the room now to herself, Laura flopped down on the couch and hit the remote control to turn on the 46 inch, high definition television set across the room from where she lay. It was seven in the evening, time for her favorite show, The Sopranos. With her son Nick not home and with Angela out of the room Laura felt comfortable watching this less than family fare program. As a matter of fact, Laura liked to fantasize that the lead female actress in the show was actually portraying Laura's real life story.

Laura was 42 years of age, just two years younger than her husband Tony. The two had met while attending Western Illinois University where Tony graduated with a business degree. At the time of his graduation Laura was just finishing up her sophomore year. Times were good then and Tony had an immediate offer for a position paying a very competitive salary that he immediately accepted.

Rather than be apart from one another, the two decided to get married and that Laura would continue her education at an institution near where the two would make their first home together.

The continuing education part of the plan did not work out, however. Within a few months of their marriage young Nicholas was on the way, followed less than two years later with the birth of Angela. Raising two youngsters and maintaining a home simply took precedence over college enrollment. As the years slipped by the desire to complete college just didn't square with the amount of effort it would require.

Despite the demands placed upon her by young motherhood, Laura did not dispense with keeping up her physical fitness and strikingly attractive appearance. Fortunately the money coming into the house also permitted her to keep abreast of the latest fashions as well.

If nothing else about Tony, she loved the fact that he wasn't into managing money. As long as he had a wad of money to flash around, he was content. He simply turned things over to Laura and assumed everything was being taken care of in good time. She had no idea what Tony did with his money, and apparently he didn't care what she did with the rest of it. She couldn't remember the last time he looked at a credit card bill or a bank statement.

About half way through the program she was watching, Tony wandered back into the room and headed straight for the bar. As he mixed himself another drink he asked, "How many of those dagos have they wiped out tonight?"

Laura simply ignored him.

With no response, Tony said, "I'll be in the kitchen watching the ball game. Don't forget that I need to talk with you yet this evening."

Despite her efforts to do so, Laura found it difficult to concentrate on the show.

"What's the big deal," she wondered. "Maybe his boss got fed up with him and canned him?" "Or, maybe the jerk quit?" "A divorce?" Her mind swirled to the point that she had no idea of what was taking place on the screen in front of her. Any of those three things would be devastating to her lifestyle.

Their relationship had certainly cooled off over the years, "but doesn't that happened to everyone." she mused. "Unless I have been totally asleep I don't think things have gotten that bad. We still share the same bed, and use it for more than sleeping fairly regularly.

"Well," she thought to herself, "I can't do anything about his job, but if it's a divorce he's planning, he'll pay through the nose, that's for sure."

Out in the kitchen Tony munched on his Whopper with cheese while washing down some of the fries with the second Rob Roy he had just whipped up.

No conversation took place between Tony and his daughter. Angela was totally occupied with trying to eat with one hand while texting with the other.

"Whatever happened to family life?" Tony wondered. "Here I am in my own home and I can't talk with my wife, and my daughter ignores me because she has to concentrate on pecking at a telephone. People used to actually do things together while at home, you know family stuff like watching a TV program together. Families played games like Monopoly, or worked on jigsaw puzzles together."

"Now everyone is in his own cyber world. People today play games on the computer, send e-mails rather than write letters, text in shorthand, or take photographs with a telephone. No wonder the family unit seems to be a thing of the past. And I'm just as guilty in contributing to the demise of the family."

"We have four television sets in the house, two computers and a game console. All four of us carry cell phones, and rarely do anything as a family anymore. This whole thing really sucks," was the last thing that went through his mind as he was drawn back to the baseball game that was on the television set in front of him.

One of the players had hit a homerun with two men on base. Unfortunately a player on the opposing team hit the ball. "The Cubs suck too," he thought to himself.

At that moment his son Nicholas came into the kitchen. As usual there came a grunt of acknowledgement from the 17 year old. Angela noted his entrance with a wave from her hand that wasn't occupied by her texting a critical message at the moment.

"It's a little late, where have you been?" Tony queried.

"Working" was the extent of Nick's reply.

"Where did you park the heap?"

"It's not a heap, Dad, it's my car" Nick replied, evidencing a bit of irritation in his voice.

"Sorry, have some of the fine supper your mother prepared for us."

u

Earlier that day, just after the confrontation with Tony, the two IRS agents enter their vehicle and began the drive back to their office.

"Well what do you think?" Jack inquired.

"It's pretty obvious that the guy is no soft touch. I think he's pretty sharp," offered Jim the other partner in the investigation. "For example, he knew right away to get his mouthpiece into the game."

"Yep, and he sure doesn't come across as a wimp," Jack followed up.

"Good! These wise guys always make things more interesting. It sort of takes the fun out of things when the target caves in right off the bat."

"I think we have this guy's ass in a box and all we have to do is nail down the lid, and it's all over for Mr. Hotshot."

"No doubt, but don't lose sight of the fact that putting this asshole behind bars isn't the real reason we were asked to take on this assignment," Jack commented and then uttered, "Damn, I hate this shit."

"What shit? I love stepping on scum like our friend Tony," Jim said with surprise in his voice.

"No, I'm talking about this traffic. It's the same crap everyday no matter where we are in the city or suburbs. What the hell happens with all of the gas taxes people pay? I thought it was to pay for better roads."

Maybe we should be investigating the politicians that handle all that money instead of chasing punks like Tony Boy."

"Man would that be great. Shit, I'd work day and night and on weekends to nail some of those pompous fat cats. Unfortunately we work for the IRS and it seldom gets involved with the political cases. It's only when some bastard has taken a bribe and then doesn't report the income to us. Often that's their downfall. If they report the bribe money on their tax return they admit their guilt. And if they don't report the money they can get nailed for income tax evasion. It's just like the box we think our Tony is in. And if we are correct, he's just a small-timer," concluded Jack as they pulled into the parking lot of the building where Jim had left his car when arriving at work that morning.

Jim exited the car and before closing the door wished Jack a good restful weekend.

u

Tony was still in the kitchen at a quarter of ten when the Cubs game came to a merciful end: Brewers 10, Cubs 2. Tony wasn't even upset with the results on the scoreboard; he was becoming accustomed to these one-sided endings for his team in what was well on its way to being one of the worst baseball seasons for Chicago in many, many years.

Tony turned off the television and the lights in the kitchen. He headed for the family room thinking that now he could finally speak with Laura about his encounter with the IRS agents earlier in the day. Both of the kids had retired to their rooms so he and his wife could speak candidly.

As he entered the family room he was immediately struck by the fact that the only light in the room was emanating from the television set. No other lights were on, and at first he couldn't see his wife. As he moved further into the room he spotted Laura, dead to the world on the sofa from which she had been watching the television show earlier in the evening.

"Great," he thought to himself. "It's so reassuring to know that my wife is so concerned and anxious to discuss a problem with me."

First Tony called his wife's name, but Laura didn't stir. Next he walked over and gently shook her by the shoulder. Laura moved about to change her sleeping position, but didn't wake up. Finally, Tony gave Laura a rather strong nudge and loudly said, "Laura, wake up!"

To this last attempt Laura responded saying, "What do you want?" "What time is it?"

"It's time to get your butt up so we can talk about the problem I mentioned to you earlier. This is serious stuff, so sit up and listen."

Laura was not impressed. "Yeh, I bet it's serious. Getting my beauty rest is serious stuff too, so it better be a big deal."

"Listen sweetie, if things go the way they might go you'll have plenty of time to watch the boob tube and get your beauty rest too," Tony emphasized in his answer to her apparent lack of interest in the topic at hand.

"What the hell is that supposed to mean?"

"I told you when you came home earlier that I had something to discuss with you."

"Well, when I was leaving my last stop this afternoon two guys approached me and said they wanted to talk with me. Turns out the guys were agents from the IRS, the Internal Revenue Service." They wanted to discuss our income tax returns with me."

"I told them to get lost, but believe me, that is not the end of it."

"Unless you have forgotten my dear, I don't know shit about that stuff. Every year you bring me a form, point to an X, hand me a pen, and say sign here. So I sign."

"Guess what, my dear, when you signed at the X you joined the game, so you better be interested in what's going on. Ever hear the saying, ignorance of the law is no excuse? You may well receive a visit like the one I had. If you do, the response is, talk to my lawyer, got it?"

"Sure know how to screw up a weekend don't you."

"Hey, don't blame me. I didn't ask for the visit from those creeps. Do you think I'm enjoying this? As a matter of fact I'm a little scared. You may recall from things you have read or movies you have watched, these people sent the infamous Al Capone to jail. This is no laughing matter," Tony said in an attempt to impress upon his wife the seriousness of the situation.

"Why are you scared, what do we have to hide anyway?"

I'd prefer not to answer that. The less you know the better. Stick to your story, which is I just sign the returns, OK?"

"Oh, one more thing. Don't make any sudden moves while talking to these guys," Tony added as a postscript. "I think one of them is carrying a gun."

"Why don't we go up to bed and work off some of this frustration?" Tony said softly, to which he heard from Laura,

"What? Are you nuts? You just told me that I should be careful when talking to a government agent who might be carrying a gun and you want me to play nice-nice with you. No way Jose! You can put that idea to rest."

u

Surprisingly, things went rather routinely in the D'Angelo house over the weekend with barely a mention of Friday evening's discussion. Tony left for his first business call of the day at his normal time, just after 7:30 that Monday morning.

Shortly thereafter the two teenagers departed for school, Nick in his "heap" while Angela wandered to the corner to wait for the school bus. Angela could ride to school with her brother, but preferred to ride the bus. Although she was a twitter of the first degree, there were still some conversations that required the emotions that the electronic world had not yet been able to integrate into the limited characters allowed for while twittering.

Laura, as was her usual custom, awoke and got up just after 8:30. Laura's philosophy was that the three other members of the household were old enough to shift for themselves. None of them were babies any longer so there was no need to make breakfast or pack lunches for them.

As she came down to breakfast the next step was to pour a cup of coffee from the already brewed pot sitting on the counter. One of her major duties, she thought, was to prepare the coffee maker just before going to bed each night. Then all Tony had to do in the morning was to press the "on" button.

With cup in hand, black of course, Laura moved to the breakfast counter upon which lay the morning paper. One of Tony's major duties was to retrieve the paper from the slot near the mailbox each morning. All this may seem to be a bit regimented, but it worked for the D'Angelos.

Although they lived in a suburb close to a major city, the D'Angelos only subscribed to the local, in town newspaper; you know, the kind that report on page one the fact that Mrs. Brown's dog Fifi gave birth to a litter of six puppies.

Laura didn't read every article, of course, but scanned the various captions at the head of each article. She would briefly pass over the obituaries just in case a familiar name might pop up. She hadn't yet reached the age when searching the obits for familiar names became a "must do" each day, as it does as one grows older.

One of her mandatory duties, however, was to complete the daily crossword puzzle. Doing so, Laura believed, cleared all of the cobwebs and sharpened her mind so she could deal with what lay ahead during the course of the day.

Laura's appearance in the morning was remarkably similar to what it was when she retired the previous evening. Except for her hair being a bit mussed from sleeping, and perhaps being a bit light on lipstick, she looked radiant.

Her complexion was almost flawless, and both her strict diet and workout schedule no doubt contributed to that fact. Her outlook on life, sort of a "What me worry?" attitude apparently contributed to her lack of worry lines in her brow or crows feet in the corner of her eyes. Hardly anyone would venture a guess that she was the mother of teenagers 15 and 17 years of age.

After finishing the crossword puzzle Laura removed her cup from the table and went to the sink. She rinsed the few items that were left from Tony's and the kids' start of the day and placed the items in the dishwasher. "See" she thought, "My fast food regimen for evening meals is contributing to our need to conserve energy. As it is I only have to run the dishwasher a few times a week."

Laura chuckled to herself as she closed the door to the dishwasher.

By this time an hour had passed, and it was time to get dressed for the day's outing. But before doing so Laura decided to call her best friend in the neighborhood, Caroline. She used her cell phone rather than the house's landline. Her decision to do so was based upon her thinking that Tony didn't have to know every aspect of her life. Even though Tony rarely looked at the bills, Laura preferred that he not see all of the numbers to which she had placed calls.

After a few rings Caroline answered the telephone.

"Didn't wake you up did I?" Laura began the conversation.

"Actually my masseuse was just finishing up when your call came so I can give you a few minutes from my busy schedule."

Laura went on with the conversation, "How generous of you. I wonder if you might sneak in an hour or so to have lunch with me today?"

"Well, let me see. "It looks like I can work in about an hour between one and two. How does that sound?"

"That's perfect. I'm heading to the health club this morning, but I should be finished by around noon. How about meeting me at Maxime's around one?"

"Forget Maxime's, I'll go for Denny's or Burger King. Take your pick" Caroline said forcefully.

"Okay, Burger King at one is it, see you then." said Laura as she hit the end button on her phone.

Laura rose from her chair and walked toward the stairway that led to the second floor of the house. At the bottom of the stairs she laid her cell phone on the credenza in the front foyer and began to ascend the stairs. While doing so she thought to herself, "What am I, some kind of a Wacko? I'm about ready to head to the health club for a workout and I just agreed to meet my best friend at Burger King. I swear I will only browse at the salad bar. Caroline sure keeps her figure and I never have been able to convince her to join the club. Maybe there is something to this housework thing."

u

Tony was in the middle of his second business call of the day when his cell phone blared out, *Ta Dot Ta Da*, similar to what one hears at the ballpark. Tony had been a jock in high school, lettering in cross-country, basketball and track. He had been a decent athlete, but not good enough to earn a scholarship to his alma mater, Western Illinois University. That not withstanding, Tony still managed to make the cross-country and track teams in college.

Tony asked his customer to excuse him, and he walked to the other side of the client's office and answered the call. "Yeah," Tony offered with his customary way of answering the telephone.

His attorney Donald Roberts, Jr. was on the other end of the call. "Good morning" he began, and then backed up. Let me restate that, hello Tony. Based on a telephone conversation I just fielded I'm not sure it is a good morning."

"Let me guess, you just talked to a geek from the IRS. Am I right?" Tony spoke softly into the telephone.

"Geeks, nerds, number-crunchers, or whatever you wish to call them, I think this could be serious. The agent said he had already spoken with you, but that you told him you wouldn't meet with them unless I was present. Is that accurate?"

"So what do you want to do?"

"Set up a meeting. As you know my job provides me with a great deal of freedom from a time perspective. So set up a meeting that's convenient for you, but the sooner the better. I want to get these guys off my back as soon as possible." Tony instructed his lawyer.

"Okay, I'll do that, but before I let you go let me ask you a few questions. Do you have any idea what might have prompted this inquiry?"

"I don't have a clue."

"Did you answer any of their questions they asked you?"

Tony said that the only thing he agreed to was that he was who they thought he was.

u

Tony's lawyer then told Tony to just standby until the arrangements for a meeting were made. I will call you when a meeting is scheduled. "I repeat as strongly as I can Tony, do NOT talk to the agents again unless I am present. Got it?"

"Got it, talk to you later." Tony said as he turned off his phone.

Having completed his telephone conversation with his lawyer, Tony turned back to his customer.

"According to your reports business has dropped off quite a bit. That's not good."

"Right on. I think it's the economy. I've never seen anything like this before," noted his customer.

"Strange. "You would think that with being unemployed people would have more time to hang out. Some of my customers are actually showing an increase in the weekly take."

"It also seems that the people who feel down and out decide to invest some money in chasing after the big score. Know what I mean?"

"Then we find a few customers that begin to think that they're a part of the company. They get a little goofy in counting the weekly cash flow. They'll start counting like this; one for you and one for me; then two for you, and one, two for me. Sort of like the old Abbot and Costello movies.

A major problem is the boss doesn't think such actions are very funny."

"In those cases we just send a few guys from our in-service training crew to the customer's joint. Generally one session to reinforce the business practices usually gets the job done."

"And of course, sometimes a few bookkeeping errors were made. In those cases the customer is given a few weeks to get his books in order and his account with the company up to a current status. Are you following me in all of this?" Tony concluded.

"Oh yeah, I'm with you every step of the way. I think I'll ask my wife to go over the books again. She's pretty good with numbers, but, hey, nobody's perfect. Right?" George the customer quickly offered.

"Sounds like a good plan. Can I enter your standard order of two cases of Ice Max as usual?" Tony said while reaching for his order pad.

"Absolutely, in fact let's, make it three cases this time."

With a thank you for the order, Tony left for his next stop, which was a luncheon appointment with his boss.

u

Tony parked his car across the street from Louie's Café and entered the restaurant. He quickly scanned the tables and booths and spotted his boss, Joey Bilotto, seated in a booth near the right rear corner of the eatery. Waving off the hostess, Tony made his way back to where Joey was waiting.

Before taking a seat Tony extended his hand and said, "Great to see you big guy."

Joey took Tony's hand in a strong grip and responded, "Me too, and it's good to see you know how to keep time. Have a seat."

Tony's boss, Joey was a man in his late 50's, rather unremarkable in appearance. He was about five feet eight inches tall and weighed perhaps a hundred and seventy pounds. Rather than describe him as being "stocky", the word burly might be more appropriate. His hair had thinned to the point where all of it that remained was the fringe above his ears.

About the only thing that might make his appearance remarkable was the ever-present half smoked cigar he held in the corner of his mouth. Tony could not recall a time, except when Joey was eating or drinking something, that the cigar was not present. Tony marveled at how clearly Joey could speak despite holding that cigar butt in place at the same time.

The get together began with the usual small talk; how's the family, how are you feeling, what did you think of the Cubs loss, etc.

Orders were given to the waitress, which did not include any drinks other than iced tea. Drinking hard liquor, or even beer for that matter, was a no-no as far as Joey was concerned, at least during working hours.

Joey's philosophy was that like drinking and driving, drinking and conducting business were likely to have the same outcome, and almost always those outcomes were not good. One had to be in full control of one's mental faculties if one was to succeed in the task at hand. In Joey's line of work success was expected, and failure was not an option.

"Let's get down to brass tacks," Joey began. "There seems to have been a rather large drop off in the income you have been reporting to the office. We're a bit concerned about that."

"I know. As a matter of fact just this morning I had a long discussion with one of my customers about that very thing. He suggested that the drop off was due to the poor economy, but I'm not totally sold on that theory."

"I'm not buying it either. The cash flow from your territory is down considerably when compared with other territories. Unless I'm mistaken, the recession is nation-wide and not just in your territory."

Immediately Tony responded, "You got that right. That's why I didn't buy the guy's excuse. I gave him a rather thorough review of our procedures when business takes an unexpected dive. I'm sure he got the message."

The waitress arrived with the lunches that had been ordered and asked if anything else was needed. Joey said everything was just fine, and asked for the check. Tony reached for the bill, but Joey waved him off and said, "This one's on me."

After having taken a bite from the sandwich he had ordered, Joey resumed the conversation. "You know Tony, some guys think that because we are essentially a cash business that not many records exists. Occasionally some wise guy figures he can beat the system, so he lets his greed outweigh his common sense."

"At first it's nickels and dimes. Then when nothing happens it become quarters and half dollars. It's like a sickness, or being like a drug addict. There's always a craving for more and more. And like addicts do, the person throws all caution to the wind."

"Then delusional thinking sets in. The wise guy figures that stealing from one's employer isn't a crime, and in his line of business there is no way he's going to be turned over to the cops. He figures he's home free. Big mistake, my friend."

Tony had been listening intently to Joey's remarks, but only picked at the lunch he had ordered.

"You started by calling these characters wise guys. I think it makes more sense to call them dumb shits."

"Greed is the most deadly of the seven deadly sins. It's amazing some of the stories you read in the paper, guys making millions getting in trouble because they had to steal just a little more. I just don't get it."

"You are right about that." Joey added. "Ever wonder what happened to the guy who had your territory before you took over?"

"The only thing I ever heard was that the guy got sick or something."

"Actually, the guy seems to have had some kind of accident. His legs were injured so he wasn't able to drive his car anymore. Of course that meant he couldn't get around to visit his customer. A real shame!"

With that the luncheon meeting was concluded and the two went their separate ways.

u

As Laura drove into the Burger King parking lot she spotted her friend Caroline walking toward the door to the restaurant. "Great," she thought, "no time wasted waiting for a lunch partner."

She gave a brief toot of the car's horn and waved to Caroline who turned and looked in the direction from which the sound came. She recognized Laura's car and gave a wave in return, then stepped inside the restaurant to wait for Laura.

Caroline was dressed rather modestly in a pair of well-worn jeans and a tee shirt. She wore flip-flops and no makeup. High fashion and glamour were rather far down Caroline's list of priorities. The top items on her list were being a wife, mother and housekeeper, in that order. Even simple outings such as today's luncheon were the exception rather than the rule for Caroline.

The Burger King parking lot offered no place where a car could be parked in the shade, so Laura parked in such a way that the front of the car was not facing into the sun. She cracked the windows just a bit to let in some air, or rather, let out some of the hot air that would build up while she was having lunch. Having done so, Laura exited her Nisan Altima and walked toward the restaurant.

In contrast to Caroline's attire, Laura wore a rather short, white skirt, and a low cut blouse in a bright yellow color. On her feet she wore a pair of obviously expensive sandals with three-inch heels. Her hair was done up in a pony tail which revealed the diamond stud earrings she always wore. A leather Coach purse was slung over her shoulder.

Once inside the door the two women greeted each other and proceeded to the line in which one stands in order to place an order for food. As she had promised herself she would do, Laura ordered what appeared to be the lowest calorie item on the menu and a diet soft drink. Caroline went the whole nine yards by ordering a Whopper with cheese and a large soda.

While waiting for their orders Laura asked, "So what's new?"

"Not a thing." Caroline responded. "You know, same old same old."

"I don't know how you stand it. Day after day the same routine, I think I would go nuts."

"Guess what, my dear? There are days when I think I am nuts, but what am I supposed to do about it? This is the life I chose to live when I married Troy. And don't get me wrong, I'm not complaining." Caroline stated, as the two picked up their orders and walked toward a booth.

Having selected a place to sit the two women alternated between taking mouthfuls of food and discussing various topics of no particular significance. Half way through the meal Laura asked what plans Caroline had for the remainder of the afternoon.

"No plans, just finish what I started this morning, and then get supper ready,"

"Well, I'm going to the Shoe when we finish up here. Why don't you come with me?"

"Shoe? What's a Shoe?"

'You know, the Golden Horseshoe Casino."

"Sorry my dear, but I can't afford the luxury of gambling. Troy and I have our hands full with bills as it is."

Laura rebutted Caroline's objection with, "Hey, it doesn't take big money to have fun. Actually you can play for pennies in the slot machines. You owe yourself an afternoon out every once in a while."

"Pennies? I've heard that song before; it starts with pennies but it doesn't stop there. Next it's nickels, then quarters, and as a last stab at getting even it's dollars. No thanks." Caroline emphatically stated her position.

"That's a lot of crap. I go three or four times a week and I'm not getting desperate enough to be into dollars."

"I'd be careful if I were you. Gambling has been the downfall of a good many otherwise successful people. It can become an addiction, like drugs. It has wiped out fortunes and ruined marriages."

"That's true, my friend, but that's not going to happen to me. I've got what you might call an insurance policy to prevent anything like that happening to me."

"That may be true, but I doubt it. I need to get back to the house."

The two left the Burger King with Caroline heading for home and Laura driving off to the "Shoe."

Late on Wednesday afternoon Tony placed a telephone call to his boss. During the brief conversation Tony explained that he would not be working the next day, Thursday, because he had an important meeting with his attorney.

His boss, Joey, had asked if the meeting was at all work-related, and Tony reassured the boss that it was not.

Upon arriving home from work that evening Tony was somewhat dismayed to find Laura waiting for him. "The stores must be closed for some reason," he thought to himself.

"Hi", Laura said as Tony entered the house. "How'd things go today?"

"Hi yourself." Tony replied. "This is an unexpected pleasure. You know, I could get used to your being here when I get home, like it was when we first got hitched." Tony uttered warmly.

"I got a call from Don Roberts this afternoon. I will be meeting with him and the guys from the IRS at 9:00 tomorrow morning. Now I will find out what this whole income tax deal is all about."

"Your attitude when I first told you about this really bothered me. This could be serious. From what I know, the IRS doesn't send people looking for you just to have something to do with their time."

"You handle the finances in this house, and as far as I know you do a good job of it. But I wonder if there is something that should have been on our tax returns that I didn't know about, investment income for example?"

Laura responded that the only investment income they had was a few dollars in interest from the bank, and that she had given that information to the person who prepared the tax returns.

"You know by now Laura that I don't get rattled too easily, but I am quite concerned about this situation. I've talked to a couple of guys who have gotten cross-wise with the IRS, and the feds can be ruthless and relentless. Have you ever heard the expression, squeezing blood from a stone? From what these guys told me, the IRS people are experts at that sort of thing."

"Oh, it can't be that bad, and besides we haven't done anything wrong, have we?"

"Not that I know of, but with the IRS things are a little different. In a court of law one is innocent until proven guilty. With the IRS one is guilty until he can prove he's innocent. Very un-American, don't you think?"

"Listen, you spend a lot of time outside of the house. You don't have a part-time job somewhere that you haven't told me about, have you?" Tony pressed Laura.

"Don't be ridiculous," Laura shot back. "You make good money, so why would I want to go to work? I don't even know how much you make. I never see your paycheck. Every few weeks you hand me some money and I put some of it in the bank. I just assumed you cashed your check, pocketed some money for your walking around money and give me the rest to use to pay the bills. Believe me, if there wasn't enough money coming in you would be the first to know."

"Look, we're just beating a dead horse. Neither of us knows what this is all about. Let's just let it drop for now and have dinner. The kids are out for the evening and I picked up a couple of nice steaks this afternoon. Go fix yourself one of your famous Rob Roys while I get dinner ready." Laura offered as she went into the kitchen.

Tony did just that, and the evening ended without any further discussion of the problem at hand.

u

The following day at 9:00 sharp, Tony entered the office of his attorney, Donald Roberts, Jr. As he did so he spotted the agents he had talked with on the previous Friday afternoon. One of the two said, "Good morning Tony."

Tony simply replied, "Yeah, right."

Tony approached the attorney's receptionists and asked that Mr. Roberts be informed that Tony had arrived for the meeting scheduled for 9:00 that morning.

The receptionist replied, "Of course, Mr. D'Angelo. May I get you a cup of coffee?"

"No thanks, I'm already coffeed out." Tony politely responded.

Tony sat on one side of the room browsing through a copy of Sports Illustrated, while the two agents occupied chairs on the other side of the room. Except for a few murmurs between the IRS agents, the room was quiet. No eye contact was made between the advisaries.

Within a few moments the intercom between the offices of the receptionist and her boss came alive. Immediately the receptionist reported that Mr. Roberts was ready to see the persons waiting in the outer office.

As Tony and the two agents moved toward the door to Mr. Roberts's office the door swung open and Don Roberts extended his hand to Tony. "Hi Tony, great to see you."

Tony shook hands with his lawyer and started into the office, but was stopped by Mr. Roberts.

"Hold it Tony. With four of us I think it's better if we meet in the conference room. Just follow me down the hall." Roberts offered.

The lawyer had not yet acknowledged the presence of the two agents, who followed along through the corridor that led to the conference room. Upon entering the room, Tony took a seat on one side of the conference table while the two agents seated themselves on the opposite side; Attorney Roberts sat at the head of the table.

"Before we get started I need to see some sort of identification from the two of you, an ID card or badge of some kind?" The lawyer began.

"Jim, one of the agents spoke up, "Badges, we ain't got no badges; we don't have to show you any stinkin badges, we're the federalies."

Attorney Roberts responded, "Very funny. You don't look old enough to remember that old Humphrey Bogart movie, Treasure of the Sierra Madre, wasn't it?"

Mr. Roberts went on. "I'm sorry, but this isn't a stand-up comedy audition. May I see your credentials so we can get started?"

Both of the agents presented identification cards, one of which showed the name James Madison and the other read John Adams.

Attorney Roberts jotted down the names on the legal pad on the table in front of him. "Interesting names," he began. "John Adams and James Madison, very historical aren't they? Are these your actual names?"

One of the agents replied that the names were partly accurate; the first names were real. The agent went on to say that the Service thinks it's a good idea that we try to separate our personal and professional lives, given the type of work that we do.

"I see. How should we address you, Mr. Adams and Mr. Madison?"

"Agent Jack replied that first names would be fine. "After all", he added, "this is a friendly, non-formal get together."

"Informal or not, I would like to tape record our discussion this morning. Do either of you have a problem with that?" Tony's attorney asked.

"No, go right ahead." agent Adams spoke up.

"Before we get started let me ask if anyone would like a cup of coffee or a soft drink?" the attorney began.

Neither of the agents nor Tony asked for refreshments, but one of the agents asked to be excused to use the restroom. With that, both of the agents left the room.

While the agents were out of the room Tony's lawyer spoke softly to Tony. "I know you must have given this matter a lot of thought since last we spoke. Did anything pop into your head as to why we are sitting here this morning?"

"Hell yes I've thought about it a lot, but I'm still in the dark."

"Did you discuss it with Laura?"

"Yep, and she says she has no idea either." was all Tony could offer.

"Okay, then. We will let these two guys do most of the talking and see where it takes us," Mr. Roberts concluded as the two agents returned to the room.

Lawyer Roberts then picked up the telephone and buzzed his receptionist to ask they he not be disturbed while he was meeting with his client unless it was an extreme emergency. Holding the telephone away from his mouth he asked the agents if they wished to receive any calls during the meeting. Both agents said no, they did not expect to have a need to answer calls.

"Hold all calls." Roberts instructed his receptionist, and then placed the telephone receiver back on its cradle.

u

On the previous Monday afternoon, shortly after waving goodbye to her friend Caroline, Laura drove up to the valet parking area of the Golden Horseshoe Casino. As she stepped out of her car the parking attendant approached with her claim check and greeted her by name.

"Hi Laura, gonna have a hot streak today?"

"Hi Jim, I sure hope so. Things have been a bit rough lately. Got any hot tips?"

"I'm afraid not my friend. If I had any inside dope I wouldn't be out here in the heat parking cars."

"That doesn't surprise me. I haven't had a winning day in weeks. You know, up a few bucks here and there, but in the end the house is the only one smiling at the end of the day. But today is going to be different. If you're still here when I leave I'll point you in the right direction." Laura reassured the attendant.

With that Laura entered the casino and headed for her favorite bank of dollar slots, The Blazing 777's.

She picked out one of the machines and fed it a $100 bill. All was set for a winning session she thought, as she hit the spin wheel. Again and again she pressed the wheel and watched in anticipation for the payoff. At three dollars per spin it took less than five minutes to work her $100 bet down to a single dollar.

"I guess this baby just needs to be warmed up a bit." She thought to herself as she fed another "Ben Franklin" into the machine.

Part way through that investment Laura hit for a $200-winner.

"That's more like it. I knew today would be the big day," she thought as she looked at the now $260 in credits showing in the money register.

Unfortunately for Laura, that $260 quickly dissipated. She changed machines and followed the same procedure for the remaining two hours of her stay. Again, the results were the same.

It was time for Laura to leave for the day, but she vowed to herself that she would be back and that the next time things would be different.

Laura had burned through $800 that afternoon.

As soon as the agents had returned to the room attorney Roberts turned on the tape recorder and began the meeting by asking the agents what had peaked their interest in his client, Mr. D'Angelo.

Agent John began, "We received an unsigned letter concerning your client's taxes. Normally we don't pay a great deal of attention to these things because many of them turn out to be crank letters. But this one was a bit different. The letter was addressed to our district office in Chicago, but it was postmarked in Seattle, Washington. That sort of made the letter stick out, so we decided to do a bit of a follow up."

"Do you know anyone in Seattle Mr. D'Angelo?" the agent asked.

"Not a soul. I've never been to Seattle, and the farthest west I have ever been was a trip to Yellowstone Park once."

"Perhaps you knew someone locally who later moved to the Seattle area?' the agent probed further.

"Again, the answer is no."

"So what was in the letter?" Tony continued.

"Agent Jim stated that he couldn't recall everything the writer had included, but the gist of it was that Tony was under reporting his income. That's a serious offense."

"Tony shot back, "I know that it's a serious offense. Do you think I'm stupid?"

"Of course not Tony. We know you're not stupid. That's why we think we can settle this thing without anyone going to jail."

"Hold it right there Mr. Are you trying to intimidate my client?" Lawyer Roberts cut in.

"Not at all. Not at all." Jim said emphatically.

"Look, the tax laws are complicated. Sometimes people become confused in connection with what's reportable income and what isn't. A lot of people think the proceeds from a life insurance policy are reportable as income, and of course they aren't. On the other hand if they make a profit selling a car they think that's tax free, and of course that gain is reportable. So it's easy to make a mistake when filling out a tax form."

"Those things are honest mistakes, and the result of such mistakes are not terribly burdensome. On the other hand, some wise guys think they can beat the system. Let me give you an example of how we are able to ferret out some of these crooks."

He went on, "We got a tip one time that a guy who owned a pizza joint who wasn't reporting all of his sales. Did we go ask this guy if he was filing false tax returns? Of course we didn't."

"We sent an agent to his shop to purchase a few pizzas, one plane Jane and one with the whole nine yards of toppings. But we didn't eat the pizzas. We took the pies to a food chemist who did an evaluation and came up with just how much in the way of ingredients it would take to make those pies."

"Next we paid a visit to the pizza guy and asked to see his records of purchases.

By analyzing his purchases we were able to come up with a reasonable estimate of how many pizzas he baked in a year, and guess what? The number was about double the number he reported as income. I don't mean the number of pizzas reported, but the number of pizzas times average price."

"Confronted with our calculations, the guy came clean."

"Very interesting, but I'm not in the Pizza business." Tony commented.

"Turns out one doesn't have to be in the pizza business, or any other business for that matter. We conduct what's called an Economic Reality Audit. Any idea what that is?"

"I'm afraid not. All I learned about economics in college is that it's a very imprecise science."

"Well, it works like this. We check with various agencies such as the Secretary of State of the state where the person of interest lives. That tells us what vehicles, boats, etc. that the taxpayer owns. We then check records of home sales in the taxpayer's neighborhood to obtain home values. Then we have an agent spend some time observing the taxpayer's shopping pattern, especially for such things as jewelry, clothing, etc. This step gives us a pattern of life style that indicates a certain level of income, say $75,000 per year."

"We compare that estimate with the level of income reported on the tax returns.

Let's say that examination indicates reported income of $50,000. So what do we have? A discrepancy of $25,000, so the obvious question is, where did the extra $25,000 come from?"

"Ever hear of credit cards?" Tony asked.

"Are you kidding?" one of the agents asked. "Most of the people in this country live on credit cards. That's why are economy is so screwed up. People spend more money on goodies than they need to and then wonder why they can't pay their bills."

The other agent added, "But that's not the case with you Tony. You have what we call an a-typical spending pattern. After checking with the credit bureaus and your bank we can only conclude that most of your family's spending is done with cash. In today's day and age that is almost unheard of behavior."

"No shit" Tony offered. I've talked with guys who are in up to their ears with credit card debts. As for my finances, you'll have to talk to my wife. She handles all of the bill-paying stuff in our house. I am surprised at what you have just said. I just assumed we weren't any different than Joe Average."

"Well you don't seem to be a member of the Joe Average family, Tony. Even your mortgage payments are made in cash each month. That is really weird," agent Jim added.

"Perhaps it's weird to you, but if you grew up in my father's house you wouldn't feel that way. To my dad, if you couldn't plop down the cash for a purchase you just moved on. Our family always lived in apartments because my father didn't want to be in debt for anything, not even a house. That really stuck with me; I even pay cash when I fill up my car with gas."

"This is all very interesting," attorney Roberts began. "But as far as I know there is no law against dealing in cash when conducting one's business. I often have clients who pay my fees in cash, and I don't even blink an eye when they do so."

"Of course there is no prohibition regarding dealing in cash. As a matter of fact most taxpayers file their tax returns on the cash basis. The only time cash dealings become an issue is when the cash going out appears to greatly exceed the cash coming in during a particular tax-reporting period, and that's why we are having this meeting." Agent John explained.

"I see" attorney Roberts said. "As was pointed out earlier in this conversation, not all money received by a taxpayer need be reported on a tax return. There are such things as gifts, inheritances, loans, etc."

U

You've presented an interesting premise, that is, somehow Mr. D'Angelo may have spent more money than his income tax returns suggests was possible, but that is all it is at this time, a suggestion. Do you have any hard data to support your position?"

"Not with us." Agent Jack replied.

"Well then" attorney Roberts continued, "this fishing expedition is over. When you have some hard facts to backup your suppositions get back in touch with me. I have had my client sign a Form 2848, Power of Attorney regarding this matter, and therefore all future contacts must be with my office. Thank you for your time gentlemen."

The two agents rose from their chairs and moved toward the door. "We have the message councilor. Would you like the information via the mail, or should we have another personal conversation like the one we had this morning?" agent Jack asked.

"By mail, then we will meet again if I deem such a meeting to be in order." Tony's lawyer replied.

"No problem, but I need to remind you that having a meeting or not isn't completely up to you. We don't even have to go to court to compel your client to meet with us, so let's try to keep this whole thing at a reasonable level of cooperation. That generally works out best for all concerned."

When the two were alone Tony asked, "What do you think? Are these guys just fishing?"

"No Tony, I don't think they are just fishing. If they were the process would probably all be started with a friendly letter from the IRS. They think they are on to something worth investing some time an effort in, something with a big payoff." Roberts answered Tony's inquiry.

Tony followed up with, "So what's next? What do I do?"

"You do nothing, and tell your wife to do nothing, and that means talking to no one about this entire thing. You'll hear from me when the next step is to be taken. In the mean time go about business as usual."

Early that evening, while gnawing on Kentucky Fried Chicken, another chef's masterpiece in the D'Angelo home, Tony began to fill Laura in on the meeting with the IRS agents.

Shortly into the discussion he asked, "What the hell's with all this paying everything with cash?"

"I don't pay everything in cash!" Laura snapped back.

"Well most things." Tony went on.

'It's just easier. When I go to the bank to make a deposit I make the mortgage payment. I just figure it makes no sense to put money in the bank, and then just turn around and write a check to take the money out again. I pay the telephone and utility bill using the computer."

"When I go shopping I don't want the hassle of entering PIN numbers or having to drag out identification in order to use a check. And don't forget what you told me about using credit cards."

"Are you trying to kid me, Laura? The way you shop I'm sure every store clerk within a fifty-mile radius knows you on sight, except for Walmart, of course. Have you ever been in a Walmart?" Tony added to the exchange.

"Very funny dear, of course I've been in Walmart, and Kmart too for your information. Those are stores I go to when I need to buy you something!" Laura shot back.

Tony went on to explain," that's part of the problem the IRS has with us. Most people today don't deal in cash. And our bank statements don't show much money moving in and out of our account. Their issue is that we are spending a lot of money we don't seem to have."

"Of course that's bull shit. How the hell can you spend money you don't have?"

"You can't, but the government wants to know why we didn't tell them about the money," Tony said as he took another swig on his Rob Roy.

Laura, as was her style replied, "Well dear, the ball is back in your court. As I told you before, you give me the money and I do my job. And when you tell me to sign here, I sign here."

"And as I told you before, when you signed the form you bought into the game. Oh, and by the way, I've thoroughly enjoyed this gourmet meal you prepared this evening." Tony offered as he left the room and headed for the bar in the family room.

"Go ahead, drink your problems away." Laura shouted to Tony as he left the room.

u

In the middle of the following week Tony received a telephone call from his boss, Joey.

"We need to get together, and soon." his bossed told Tony.

"Whenever you say Joey, you're the man."

"Yeah, I know, and that's why I'm telling you the meeting will be Friday for lunch at the same place we met last time. We did some checking on some of the units you service with your customers. I'm sure you will be greatly interested in our findings. Don't be late." And with that Joey ended the conversation.

"Wonderful!" Tony thought to himself as he returned his cell phone to the holster on his belt. "I don't have enough to sweat out with those IRS goons bugging me. Now I have to meet with Joey and listen to what I'm sure is not going to be good news. As always, good news can wait, but for bad news it's always urgent."

Tony's compensation had declined in recent months, but again he had attributed that to the economy. He began to go through his customer list. As he drove to his next business stop he rolled over various facts in his mind, but nothing popped up as being unusual.

Tony had worked for the Ice Max Company for just over four years and had the same territory during all of those years. His customers were all retail outlets, mostly mom and pop, local taverns. Of course ownerships had changed from time to time, but the businesses he served remain pretty much the same over time.

His last call of the day was at Jed's Place, a typical small-time gin mill in a far south suburb of Chicago. As Tony parked his car in front of the place, it occurred to him that a new owner now ran Jed's Place. An old timer who retired about six months ago had sold the place. Reflecting on this situation for a few moments Tony remembered that sales had taken a dive since the change of ownership.

However, considering the circumstances involved in the sale, Tony had not found the change in the level of business to be all that unusual. The new owner of Jed's Place, Lamar, was black. A good number of the Jed's Place patrons were along in years themselves, and rubbing drinking elbows with people of color was not something to which they had taken well.

"Some things just don't change." Tony thought to himself.

Tony entered the establishment and was immediately greeted with, "Hey, it's my main man Tony! I been expecting you and got the paperwork all set, and it's in this here envelope. Have a seat and let me get you a cool one." Lamar Bowers offered.

"I'll take the seat, but I'll pass on the cool one, unless it's a Coke. I never mix booze and business." Tony replied.

He went on, "How's things going with you?"

Lamar moaned, "Slow man, really slow, but I'm dealin with it."

"Dealin with it? I hope you didn't say dealing in it!"

"No way, man. I ain't nuts. I got enough troubles without getting involved in that shit. Too may of the brothers are already on long vacations for dealing. I'm tired, but being in stir doesn't sound like a vacation to me."

"Good thinking my man. Sounds like you've got your head on straight, but problems? You own your own business, you have to expect problems."

"I know, I know" Lamar continued his rant. "First I get the punks coming in and trying to convince me they're old enough to be in here. Then on Friday and Saturday nights I get the sisters commin in. They sit at the bar, order one drink, and then nurse it for a long time. From time to time they will get up and sashay back and forth to the ladies room, hoping to attract some interest, of course."

He went on, "And of course I have the screwballs come in and try to talk me into giving them some take-out beer for food stamps. I'm telling you man, this is no easy way to make an honest living."

"It beats working for somebody else doesn't it?" Tony said unsympathetically.

"You're all heart man!"

"Well, I have to be hitting the road, but before I leave let me ask you a question. Seems like your monthly business has tapered off quite a bit from what the former owner was doing. Any reason for that?" Tony inquired.

Lamar responded that he thought it might just be due to having a younger crowd coming in to his place.

Tony countered that he had other clients who seemed to draw a wide variety of

Customers, including the younger crowd, to their joints, and that fact didn't seem to have any effect the level of business he was accustomed to seeing.

"Well that may be," Lamar offered. "But most of the regulars that come in here think they're going to hit it big with the lottery, so they don't seem to be interested in just getting ahead a few bucks at a time. They're goofy if you ask me. What are the chances of hitting the lottery, a million or more to one?"

"Those people don't think like you and me." Tony offered. "They aren't acquainted with the idea that work and savings result in financial comfort. They think the world is against them, and the only way to get better is to hit the big one. I guess they don't buy the old saying, 'no pain, and no gain'. Of course that thinking isn't limited to your customers."

"I've got acquaintances who think they are entitled to have all of the goodies in life right now. Working hard and moving up the economic chain doesn't appeal to them. I call them members of the 'I want it now generation.'"

"But it's getting worse. The next generation, like my kids, makes up what I call the 'I'm entitled to it' generation'. Do see what I'm saying, Lamar?"

"I'm with you, man. I see that crap in my younger customers all the time. I got guys coming in here bitching and moaning that their unemployment payments are running out. And some of the sisters are all in an uproar because their welfare or food stamp allowances are being cut back."

"I tellim; Get a job, and they act like I'm nuts. I have never taken a dime of government money except for a few bucks to help me to get my GED certificate. Of course I don't complain if it's the government's money that those losers are throwing over the bar."

"Oh, by the way," Lamar continued, "A couple of your guys were in last week to check on the equipment. They didn't say much, but I guess they found everything in order. Nice guys, but they didn't talk much."

"That's no surprise. The company pays them to check on equipment and make reports, not to shoot the shit. See you next week," and with that Tony left Jed's Place.

Upon entering his car, Tony checked his cell phone for messages and missed calls. One of the messages was from Laura who indicated that she would be late for dinner, and asked Tony to feed himself and the kids with a pizza that he would find in the freezer in the basement.

"Why text me with this crap?" thought Tony. "It would make more sense for Laura to send an email to say she would be home for dinner."

There were three more messages: The first was from his daughter, Angela, explaining that volleyball was going to keep her at school later than usual. The next message was from his son, Nick, who left the message that he had to work late. The kids had become accustomed to the fact that their mother was rarely home at mealtime.

The third message was from a customer who said that he had an equipment failure and asked what he should do about the problem.

After checking his address book, Tony called the customer and informed him that he should do nothing, except wait for the repairman. Messing with the equipment could definitely lead to problems, Tony reminded the customer.

Tony then started his car and began the drive home.

u

Earlier that same day, just after one in the afternoon, Laura's telephone rang. She rummaged through her purse, pulling the phone out just in time. One more ring and the call would have gone to voice-mail hell. The call was from her friend Caroline.

"Hi," Laura said in a cheerful voice. "What prompts this surprise?"

"Where are you?" Caroline inquired.

"I'm in Macys over at the mall. Just grazing, as Tony would call it. He tells people I don't go shopping; I go grazing or foraging. According to him, he's the hunter in the family and I'm the gather. So why'd you call me?"

Caroline began, "Well it's Friday afternoon and I've been busting my butt in this house all week. I got to thinking about what you said at lunch the other day; you know, that I need to get out a little more."

So I called my mother-in-law and she agreed to come over and be here for the kids when they get home from school. I'm ready to go, so what do we do?"

"It'll take me about twenty minutes to get to your place. Can you be ready by then?"

"I think so." Caroline replied. "But what should I wear. Where are we going?"

Laura explained that casual dress would be fine, and that they were going to the casino.

"The shoe's the only place to go when you need to get away from the real world. See you in a few minutes." Laura said, smiling as she returned her phone to her purse.

After picking up Caroline the two drove for just under 30 minutes, Laura pulled into the valet parking area of the Golden Horse Shoe Casino. After exiting from the vehicle the two women entered the casino. Laura immediately headed for the VIP desk with Caroline close behind.

As they approached the VIP hostess came to an alert position and greeted Laura and her companion.

"Good afternoon Mrs. D'Angelo. How are you on this fine day." The hostess greeted Laura.

"Well, thank you, very well. This is my friend Caroline."

"Glad to meet you. Now what can I do for you today Mrs. D'Angelo" the hostess asked.

Laura explained that because this was her friend's first visit, the afternoon would be mostly spent just wondering around. Therefore I suppose about $500 would get the job done.

The hostess asked for Laura's VIP Card and swiped the card through the card reader. Laura was then asked to enter her PIN to verify the transaction. Having done so, Laura was given $500 in 50 dollar bills. She handed two of the bills to Caroline and said, "My treat."

Caroline was awe struck by what she had just witnessed. The two women left the desk of the hostess and wandered out on to the floor of the casino and into the sounds emanating from the banks of slot machines.

Caroline grabbed Laura by the elbow and inquired, "What the hell was that all about? You just walk in, say hello, stick out your hand and somebody puts $500 in it? I don't get it?"

"I'll fill you in later. You have to have connections and make arrangements. If you do you can minimize your losses and maximize your chances of coming out on top. Let's start to see if this is your lucky day. Here's a bank of dollar machines that I like to play." Laura said while pointing to the blazing sevens machines.

"Whoa, you said I could gamble pennies. No way am I going to start dumping in money a dollar at a time." Caroline balked.

Laura explained that actually it was three dollars at a time because you had to play three coins if you expected to win big. To which Caroline responded that was too rich for her blood, and insisted on finding the penny machines.

And so the two of them wandered over to the casino section that housed the penny slot machines. Caroline picked out one that looked "cute" and began her gambling adventure.

However, in a short period of time she figured out that gambling pennies was a real misnomer. In order to win any real money the player had to feed pennies to multiple lines showing on the machine's screen. Doing so could amount to as gambling as much as 90 cents per push of the button. So much for gambling with pennies she thought.

While Caroline was feeding the penny machines Laura had walked back to the blazing sevens and began feeding the dollars the machines. Her luck was a bit better this time, and after a few hours she found herself up a couple hundred dollars.

Just before six o'clock she walked back to where Caroline was playing and asked, "How's it going?"

"Not so hot, I'm afraid. I feel bad because I lost about $50 of your money."

"No big deal. It's part of the game. Hungry? Laura asked.

"Yeah, a little, but it's getting late. Shouldn't we hit the road?"

"No way, I'm on a roll today. I called Tony and told him not to expect me for supper and what to do to feed the kids. So we're free for the evening. Let's go eat. They have a great buffet here." Laura coaxed Caroline.

The two women approached the entrance to the buffet where a long line of patrons who were waiting to be admitted. Laura walked passed the people who were waiting and went to an area just to the side of the buffet cashier's position.

Laura showed the person at that station her identification card and the two women were immediately admitted.

Caroline was impressed. Again she asked, "What was that all about?"

"Simple." If you are a player the casino appreciates it and shows it's thanks by giving you a few perks. Of course they're not all big-hearted softies. They know very well that if you have any freebies coming you'll be back to claim them, and of course you'll gamble every time you show up. They also like to play on your ego. But so what? Let's eat." Laura said as she steered Caroline toward the stack of dishes at the beginning of one of the serving lines.

After filling their plates with a modest amount of food the two women found an unoccupied table in the corner of the room the ladies began to enjoy the sumptuous meal. A short time later Caroline noticed a rather dapper looking man, dressed in a suit and tie enter the room and begin to look about as if searching for someone.

u

T hen he seemed to stop and focus on the table at which she and Laura were sitting. He then waved in her direction and began walking toward the table. Out of the corner of her eye Caroline thought she saw Laura raise her hand and make a gesture similar to a school-crossing guard doing so to stop traffic. The gentleman immediately came to a stop, paused for a moment, then turned and left the room.

"Curious." Caroline thought to herself, and then went on to enjoying the crab legs she had selected on her first pass through the many food items available on the buffet.

Her friend Laura seemed to Caroline to be a bit nervous all of a sudden.

So Caroline asked, "What's the matter? You seem a bit tense. Do you feel alright?"

Laura assured her companion that everything was fine, and that she perhaps had eaten something that didn't agree with her. She then asked to be excused for a few minutes while she went to the ladies room.

In a short period of time Laura returned to the table and asked Caroline if she was ready to hit the machines again. Caroline responded yes, but only for a little while.

Over the next few hours the two plied their luck on several different machines, and it seems that Lady Luck was with both of them this time. As they left for the valet parking area Caroline announced that she had one 75 dollars and offered to give Laura back the $100 she had staked Caroline with at the outset of the day.

"No way, that hundred was a gift, and the rest you won fair and square. See, I told you this could be a lot of fun. I bet you haven't given one thought to your housework during the past several hours." Laura said with a big smile on her face.

Caroline admitted that in fact she hadn't worried about anything except what symbols the machine's wheels would stop at.

"I haven't had this much fun and relaxation at the same time in quite a while. Thanks."

u

Immediately after dropping Caroline off in front of her house, Laura drove to a nearby McDonalds restaurant and went in for a cup of coffee. After receiving her order Laura found a seat in a sparsely occupied section of the place and sat down.

She immediately removed her cell phone from her purse and dialed a number.

After a few rings a male voice on the other end of the call said, "Hi Babe, I've been hoping you would call. You acted a bit upset when I saw you earlier."

"Don't Hi Babe me! Are you some kind of moron, or are you getting Alzheimer's? How many times have I told you that you are not to approach me if I'm with someone else at the casino?"

"Yeah, yeah, I know, but I get anxious whenever I see you."

Laura shot back, "No Ross, you don't get anxious, you get stupid. Two parties to an arrangement can keep things to themselves. As soon as a third person gets in on the deal all bets are off. People like to talk, Ross."

"I like you Ross, and I think I give you what you need. Don't spoil things."

"We have a nice arrangement that keeps a smile on both of our faces. You are very generous and kind to me. I think I reciprocate in kind. But don't forget, there's very little room for slip-ups. So please, be careful. If you really must talk to me, call me. OK?" Laura spoke softly into the phone.

"You're right, of course. I'm sorry. Talk to you soon," Ross responded, and then ended the call.

Ross Wellington, a man in his early 50's, leaned back in the chair he occupied in his up-scale apartment, and thought to himself: "This makes no sense. I'm a successful business owner making a lot of money. In the rest of the world I give the orders, and I just let a woman read me the riot act."

"What the hell is going on here? I'm in good physical health. Anyone with half a brain can tell that I don't wear off-the-rack suits from Sears. There are plenty of women out there that I could hook up with in a minute. So what's the deal?

The deal is, this is different," he concluded.

u

Friday, the following day, Tony arrived for his meeting at the time and place indicated by his boss during their last telephone call. He walked into the restaurant and immediately headed for the table where he knew Joey would be seated. Joey was a creature of habit so Tony was not at all surprised to see the man waiting for him.

With the usual hello and handshake Tony sat down on the opposite side of the table from where Joey was seated.

"How are things?" Tony began.

"I'm really pissed, but I'm starting to cool off."

Tony came back, "Why? What's the problem?"

Joey explained his state of mind: "See that punk over by the cash register? The asshole came up to me after I sat down here and says, sir, this is a smoke-free restaurant. So I said, so?"

So the clown says, "Well you have a cigar in your mouth." And I said so?

The guy goes on to preach to me that smoke free means no smoking.

"So I ask the jerk, do you see any smoke, and he says no. I get back in with, well then what's the problem? I read your sign and it doesn't say no chewing, and that's all I'm doing."

"But you might light it," he says.

"If and when I light it you can get on my case. Until then I suggest you go mind your own business. You might be new around here, but I'm not. Do me a favor and go ask your boss if he thinks you should be hassling me. Then come back and see me."

"I'm telling you Tony, this country is going to hell. Pretty soon it will be against the law to fart because if you do the government will be on your ass for polluting the air." So how are things with you?" Joey asked in a more calm voice.

"Fine, Joey. Just fine, except for a little rub with the IRS."

"The IRS? There's another bunch of assholes. Is it serious?"

Tony told his boss that he wasn't sure yet.

"Just keep me posted. As you can imagine, the organization isn't real keen on the idea of having to talk to the tax guys. Let's get to the matter that is the reason I asked you to have lunch today."

"We had our guys check out the equipment at one of your customer's joint the other day. It was the place owned by that spade Lamar whatever. Any idea what they found?"

Tony winced a bit when he heard Joey's description of his customer, Lamar.

He was from a different generation than his boss so using terms like spade and spic were not a part of his speech pattern.

Tony remarked, "Well, seeing as we are having this meeting I suspect that what the guys found was not good."

"Exactly. Any idea what your guy Lamar did for a living before going into his own business?"

"Not really. I know he worked someplace and got tired of taking orders. So he saved some money and decided to become his own boss. At least that's what he tells me."

"Right, up to a point. It turns out that he worked for one of the local casinos, in the maintenance department. We checked it out. He had a decent job making $22 an hour plus benefits. For a guy without an education that's not a bad deal. So why would he walk away?"

He continued, "Look making close to 50 grand a year plus benefits isn't too bad today. The odds of doing better than that running a local watering hole are like slim and none. Your pal Lamar aint no dummy, Tony. He had to have an angle that pointed to scoring a lot better. And, of course, he did."

"So what's the scam?"

"We checked with the county recorder of deeds and found out that our friend Lamar has a partner, a guy named William Brown. So our guys did some digging to see what could be learned about Lamar's silent partner. And guess what? Good old Willie works at the same casino that Lamar left. The only difference is that Willie works in the slot machine repair shop. He has been there for a number of years so this guy knows his stuff."

"You're telling me that this guy Brown has been messing with the equipment, aren't you?" Tony said softly.

"That's correct, my friend, and that doesn't make us real happy. You sure you didn't know anything about this?"

Tony replied forcefully, "Joey, that's a stupid question. You've been around the block more times than I have, but I've been in this game long enough to know where the out of bounds lines are. No way am I going to be stupid enough to get flagged for breaking the rules. So you can forget that shit!

And by the way, you keep referring to Lamar as my buddy. That's bull shit too."

"What happens now?"

"I don't know yet. The guys up the line are thinking it over. This is a funny business, Tony. We can't just call the cops and tell them one of our people is stealing from us. And just shit canning the guy doesn't make up for the losses. But that's not our problem. All we have to do is convince the brass that we weren't in on the scam. And I believe you Tony, so I guess we just wait and see what happens. For now, just go about business as usual."

"Thanks Joey. Believe me, you have no worries with me. Anything else today?"

"That's it my friend. We'll meet again when the word comes down." And with that the meeting was over.

Since it was already well past one in the afternoon Tony decided to call it a day and headed for home.

After parking his car Tony walked over to the mailbox in the front of the house to see what bills the mail carrier had left this time. As he opened the door to the box that sat atop a brick pillar at the head of the driveway Tony thought to himself, "Same old crap I suppose. All the pieces of mail we seem to get in this house are "buy me, give me, or vote for me. Just once I would like to see an actual letter from an old friend or a relative."

His thoughts continued as he reached into the box, "But that's not going to happen. Today it's all email. I wonder if they still teach kids how to write in school?"

Unfortunately for Tony there was a letter addressed to him in the day's mail. The letter was from the United States Treasury, Internal Revenue Service.

"Bad way to start the weekend," he thought.

u

After leafing through the various pieces of mail Tony had removed from the mailbox in front of his home, Tony headed for the house. He was pleased to see that his recent lecture to his daughter had apparently taken effect. He needed his key to open the front door of the home.

Leaving his keys and most of the mail on the foyer credenza, Tony headed for the bar in the family room. The letter from the IRS remained unopened. Following the usual ritual of mixing the perfect Rob Roy, Tony sat down and opened the IRS letter.

To his dismay, the form letter indicated that he owed the Government some $20,000-plus in-unpaid taxes, penalties and interest. "Holy shit," he said aloud.

Upon a closer reading of the letter he found that the tax deficiency notice related to the Year 2007. That meant the Years 2008 and 2009 might result in more letters demanding more money.

Tony gulped, and then gulped again, the second one was when he emptied half of his drink glass. Then he grabbed the phone and immediately dialed the cell phone number of his attorney, Donald Roberts.

When the phone was answered on the third ring, Tony spoke into the phone:

"Don, I just opened a letter from the IRS, and . . ."

His lawyer cut him off, "I know. I received a copy today since you signed the power of attorney form the other day."

"These guys are talking some serious money." Tony interjected.

"Don't panic Tony. The government likes to shake people up by proposing large dollar amounts. It's a gambit they use in hopes that you will lose your cool and be cooperative."

"Well it's working my friend. When I saw the figure of 20 G's I lost my cool all right. In fact I almost lost my bladder in my pants. What the hell do we do now?"

"We arrange for a meeting with them and ask them to show how they arrived at their figure. Then we attack it as being spurious, and deny the liability. I'll call them and set up the meeting. Any day and time okay with you?"

u

Tony replied that as usual his schedule was quite flexible, so whatever could be worked out was okay with him. He concluded that as far as he was concerned the sooner this thing could be resolved the better.

After hanging up the telephone Tony finished his drink and headed for the bar for a refill. Just then Laura came into the room.

She greeted Tony by saying hi, and asking how his day had gone.

"Oh just great, until I opened the mail. Take a look at that letter on the table next to my chair."

Laura picked up the letter and read its contents. "Holy shit!" she began. "How the hell could we owe that much money? And if we do, where's the money going to come from to pay it?"

"I have no idea. But I'm glad to hear you're using the word we for a change. Would you like to join me in a drink to celebrate this grand occasion?"

"No thanks. I think a couple of Advils makes more sense," she replied and headed out of the room toward the kitchen.

Tony returned to his chair with his refreshed drink in his hand. He just sat there staring at the letter.

The remainder of the weekend passed in the usual fashion, with one exception.

During his regular Saturday morning golf outing his game just wasn't up to his normal level of play. His partners chided and kidded him for poor play. Tony chose not to reveal to them the fact that he could not concentrate on his game because all he seemed to be able to think about was his impending confrontation with Big Brother.

u

The following Friday morning at 9:00 Tony arrived at his lawyer's office for the meeting with the IRS agents. Acting on Tony's request, the meeting had been arranged by attorney Roberts.

When Tony walked into the office the two IRS agents were already sitting in the office. They greeted Tony in a cordial, but rather formal manner. Tony nodded hello, and then spoke with the receptionist who indicated that she would let Mr. Roberts know that Tony had arrived.

A short time later Don Roberts exited his private office and asked the meeting participants to accompany him to the conference room where they had met the last time they had been together. Tony, his lawyer and the agents all took the exact seats they had previously occupied.

Mr. Roberts began the meeting by warmly greeting the three other meeting participants. He again asked the agents if they would have any objection to his recording the meeting, to which the IRS people said no, they had no objection.

After turning on the recorder, Mr. Roberts began:

"Well gentlemen you seem to have arrived at a figure for a tax liability for my client. Would care to explain to us how it is that you arrived at your figure?"

Agent Adams was the first to speak.

"Certainly," he said.

He then handed documents to Tony and his lawyer.

Agent Jim began. "What I have just given to you is an income tax return we have created for the year in question."

Tony jumped in, "I already filed a tax return. So what's with this new version?"

"Well Tony, we go about things a little differently than you do. Let me explain."

"When you prepare your tax returns you start with income. You then deduct certain expenses and end up with what you think is subject to income taxes. You also take deductions for dependents according to existing tax law, of course."

u

"We take what you might call a reverse approach. The return we prepare begins with a dollar-figure that we think supports the life-style you appear to have been living."

"We arrive at the figure by totaling up the amounts you pay for things like mortgage payments, car payments, property tax payments, life insurance, education expenses, etc. We then add a figure for food, routine medical care and homeowner maintenance expenses. Finally we factor in estimated expenses based upon your apparent shopping habits; the purchase of luxury items, for example.

Through this process we arrive at a figure that must have been available to you during the tax-year under review. From that figure we deduct the income reported on the tax return you filed, in your case a salary of $46,000 and a few dollars of interest income. If the income reported doesn't match our calculated income figure we assume you had income that went unreported on your return."

Attorney Roberts spoke up, "Of course your figures are all theoretical and speculative aren't they?"

"Actually they're not. We have actual numbers from your lenders and utility companies. We also have facts regarding things such as money paid to educational institutions, charitable institutions and licensing agencies. We have documents with us to support our position if you would like to see them. No Mr. Roberts, we believe our estimate of expenditures is well supported by objective evidence." Agent John assured Mr. Roberts.

He continued, "So the question remains, where did the money come from?"

"I have no idea. It seems like you have accounted for everything that my family spends."

Agent John spoke up. You'd be surprised how fast things add up. Do you have any hobbies, like playing golf for example?"

Tony said that he did indeed play golf on weekends.

"And how much are the greens fees, and how many rounds do you play in a year?"

He reported that he played about 25 weekends a year and the cost of a round was $60.

"Let's see, assuming you have a few drinks and maybe a bite to eat when you're at the course you probably drop a hundred bucks each outing. If we multiply that be 25 rounds we have $2,500, not counting any side bets, of course."

"And then there's that trip you and your golfing buddies took to South Carolina in the spring of 07. With that we can add another two thousand. Adds up fast, doesn't it Mr. D'Angelo?"

"Amazing. I have never looked at it that way." is all Tony could say.

The agent continued, "Let's see, according to your tax return you have two teenaged children. Did either of them have a job in 2007?"

Tony responded that no, neither of the children had worked that year, but now his son has a part-time job.

Tony was then asked if he and his wife gave the kids any spending money.

He replied that for doing certain chores around the house they are each given a $25 per week allowance.

Using a pencil and the scratch pad on the table in front of him the agent quickly pointed out that the allowances totaled $2,600 for a year.

"So you see, Mr. D'Angelo, with just these few things we are already up to more than $7,000 in cash outlays, and we haven't even considered things like shopping for Christmas, birthdays, back-to-school expenses or entertainment. Would you care to comment?"

Mr. Roberts spoke first. "No, my client would not like to comment at this time. How would you like my client to respond to what you have presented today?"

One of the agents said the expected response was that Tony pays the assessment.

"And if he does that, is that the end of this matter?" Roberts asked.

"Maybe yes, and maybe no. It sort of depends upon the source of the unreported income. Does your client engage in gambling activities?"

"I don't have an answer to that question, or to any other questions at this time," Don Roberts said sharply.

"My client and I will require some time before we are ready to respond. Thank you for your time this morning gentlemen. I will contact you when we are prepared to further discuss this matter." And with that, the meeting was concluded.

After the two agents left the room attorney Roberts turned to Tony and said: "This does not look good my friend. Although it's almost all speculation, I think they make a pretty sound argument in support of their position. If they can prove their contentions that you spent more than was possible based upon your tax filing, the burden of proof to refute it falls on you."

He went on, "I'm sure you have heard of attorney/client privilege. Of course that means you can tell me anything and I can't be compelled to reveal anything you have said in confidence. So the question is, where did the money come from? What about the gambling question?"

"I don't gamble, Don. Gambling's for suckers. Sure, like the guy said, there's a few side bets on the golf course, but that's it for me," Tony assured his lawyer.

"What about your wife, Laura?"

"Not as far as I know. Once in a while she'll go to one of those ladies bunko parties or a PTA bingo or something. But real gambling, I don't think so. And once in while she buys a Powerball Lottery ticket, but that's not gambling; that's throwing money away."

Don probed further, "Look Tony, my job is to help you, but I can't do that if I don't have all of the facts. Do you understand that?"

"Of course I do. Actually I do have a little side deal going. I'm just not ready to discuss that yet. I have to give it more thought. Give me a few days to think it over. Okay?"

"Okay, but let me add something. Twenty thousand might seem like a lot of money to you. But to the government it's peanuts. I think they are after something else and see you as the gateway to bigger things. Get back to me as soon as you can."

Tony left the meeting feeling fully drained of energy. While sitting in his car he took out his cell phone and dialed his boss's number.

u

After hearing the usual "yeah" on the other end of the call Tony told his boss that he was taking the rest of the day off. He described some of what went on in the meeting with the IRS agents, and concluded by saying he just needed to chill out for a while.

Joey, his boss, said he understood, and then suggested the two of them get together to discuss what Tony was going through and also the Lamar matter. Of course Tony agreed, and told the boss to just let him know when he wanted to meet.

After completing his call with the boss, Tony began the drive to his home. On the way he pulled into the drive up window of a local Taco Bell and picked up a couple of burritos. While doing so he thought to himself, "hell, I can make as good a meal as Laura usually does." and then chuckled to himself.

Upon arriving home in the early afternoon Tony immediately prioritized his actions: 1. Head for the bar in the family room, 2. Turn on the Cubs game, 3. Crap out.

When the rest of the family arrived at various times during the late afternoon and early evening Tony remained in the world of nod, apparently oblivious of his real-world problems.

But outward appearances can be deceiving to an observer. While Tony lay quite still in his relining chair, except for his breathing, his mind raced from one scene to another.

First he saw himself sitting alone in a small room. The room in which he visualized himself was quite small, and had walls made of concrete blocks. The only avenue to viewing the rest of the world was through a door that had a small bar-covered opening in it. The furnishings, unlike the family room in his home, consisted of a steel cot with a thin mattress on it, and the metal stool on which he sat. The room was damp, chilly and the air in it was rather stale.

Then, all of a sudden, he found himself sitting in a very plush office. He was sitting in a chair facing a desk. On the other side of the desk was his boss Joey. His boss was grilling him with merciless questions: "Whom did you talk to? What did you tell them? Why did you rat on us? Do you know what happens to people who fink on us?"

u

At last, after an increase in the television volume as a commercial was aired, Tony came back to the real world, with sweat dampening his brow.

Tony looked across the room to see his wife lying on the sofa.

"What time is it?" he asked.

"Not quite 9:00 o'clock; you were really sawing wood so I decided not to wake you. There's some pizza in the kitchen if you're hungry."

"No thanks. I don't feel hungry right now. I'm kind of bent out of shape after meeting with the tax guys and Don Roberts this morning."

Laura continued the conversation, "I gather things didn't go too well then?"

"That my dear," Tony went on, "is the understatement of the year! These guys are not your typical government employees. They have got their heads on straight, and they know how to dig up information. They have information from the mortgage company, the bank, the county property tax people, the schools the kids attend, and you name it."

"Here's the problem; they show how much money you spent, and then you have to show where you got the money. You can't deny that you had the money because they can prove you spent it. And if you had the money, and can't show that it came from a gift or something like that, you owe the tax, period!"

"Well, that stinks," Laura, remarked.

"Stinks out loud, but that's the way it is."

He went on, "Let me ask you a question. During the meeting the feds asked me about gambling. Of course I said that was out of the question. Was I correct? Are you doing any gambling that you haven't told me about?"

Reacting to that question, Laura sat upright on the sofa on which she had been lying.

"Gambling? Not a chance! Well, wait a minute. Sometimes my friend Caroline will call and ask me to go to the casino with her. Usually I say no, but once in a while I will go with her. But I only play pennies when I do go. Even if the government guys checked that out they wouldn't be able to run up a bill of $20,000," Laura offered as an answer to Tony's question.

"Pennies? What the hell's a penny. You can't buy anything for a penny anymore. When's the last time you saw a sign for penny candy? Too bad the IRS isn't talking about pennies."

u

The next day while Tony and his golf buddies were having a beer after their usual Saturday round of golf his cell phone rang. Upon answering he heard his boss's voice on the other end of the call.

"Tony we need to meet soon. Be at my place Monday at nine in the morning. Okay?" Tony heard is boss saying.

"No problem Joey. What's it about?"

"You'll find out on Monday. Don't plan any other business for the morning. See you then." Joey said and ended the call.

Tony put his phone away and went to chatting with his friends. As was the case while out on the golf course, Tony couldn't keep his mind off of his two problems: The IRS matter and the tone in his boss's voice a few minutes ago.

After a few more minutes of small talk, Tony excused himself and left to go home.

Upon arriving home Tony again found the place empty. Tony thought, "why the hell am I paying for this big house when there isn't ever anyone using it."

Following his customary Saturday afternoon routine, Tony headed for the bar and whipped up one of his favorite drinks, actually he made a double this time. He then sat down in his chair, flipped on the TV, changed channels until he found the ballgame, and that leaned back in the chair.

"How the hell am I going to explain the extra money?" he mused.

u

At 9:00 o'clock Monday morning Tony entered the offices from which his boss did business. The receptionist greeted Tony by name and said she would let Mr. Bilotto know he was here.

Before Tony could take a seat his boss opened the door to his office and told Tony to come in. As he entered the office his boss pointed to a chair facing the desk in the office and told Tony to have a seat.

"Well Tony, how was your weekend?"

"Not so hot. I've been thinking about our meeting this morning, and I have another major problem to deal with."

Joey came back with, "Sorry to hear that my friend. Maybe after we talk you'll feel a little better."

"If you remember, the last time we talked we were discussing the drop off in revenue from your territory. We also spoke about the guy Lamar and his partner. After some further checking it turns out that it's all connected."

"After our guys found some discrepancies with the equipment in Lamar's place we decided to check out a few other locations. And guess what? We found the same irregularities."

"Well if the problem is that wide spread I would guess whoever made the machines screwed up."

"Come on Tony, don't be stupid. We've been dealing with the same supplier for years. They're totally reliable. So we had a little heart to heart talk with our friend Lamar."

Joey continued, "Seems like Lamar boy got cozy with other owners in your territory. He told them for a small piece of the action he could increase their profits. Almost all of the greedy bastards went along with the scam. But the whole deal is history now."

"How's that?"

"I just told you. We had a little meeting with Lamar. He's decided to sell his place and try to get his job back at the casino. We told him we had a buyer for his business and made him an offer that was too good to refuse. So that's that."

"Then we had our guys go to all of the joints involved and do some work on their equipment. We charged each of them five grand for maintenance work. There were a couple of beefs, but most of them just bit the bullet and paid up.

"Oh, and by the way, his partner, the guy that fixes slot machines at the casino, he's going to be out of commission for awhile. Seems he had an accident and broke his hand. It was a real freaky kind of accident. I hear he tripped and somehow someone stepped on his hand. A real shame!"

"Man, I feel a lot better already, but still I feel a little guilty. Like I should have picked up on the scam."

"No, No, Tony, this was a clever and smooth operation. It took us longer than usual to figure it out ourselves. So just write it off to experience. Now what's the other problem you've been sweating about?"

Tony began, "It's the IRS. They're on my ass and want some serious money. They're claiming I had a lot more income than I reported on my tax return. Unfortunately, the IRS guys are right. As you know, I get a W-2 Form from you guys. So I figure; whatever it says I report. Simple, right? Wrong!"

Joey immediately replied, "Tony, Tony, Tony, you're a bright guy. I've been thinking that you had the potential to maybe go far in this business. But now I'm not so sure."

"Look" Joey continued, "If you want to you can cheat on your wife, smoke some grass, take a few snorts, or run a private poker game, but you don't mess with the government. I'm getting on in years, but even I know that with today's computer shit you can hardly hide anything. Tons of big guys have been on forced vacations because they got themselves sideways with Uncle Sam."

"What's the bite they're asking for?"

"Twenty G's, and to me that's a ton."

"You gotta pay Tony. You gotta pay'em and hope they go away."

Tony shot back, in a voice he was not accustomed to using with his boss, "yeah, and where do I come up with the money?"

"I'll work on that and get back to you as soon as I can. Have you got someone helping you with this shit?"

"Of course I have. I only meet with the feds when my lawyer is there. He's waiting for me to let him know what I want to do next. And I've told my wife to refuse to talk to anyone as well."

"Good, let's keep it that way. I'm sure we can work this thing out so just don't panic. I'll call you when I have some word from the top," Joey said, and that was the end of their meeting.

Despite not feeling like it, Tony went about his business calls for the remainder of the afternoon. In none of the stops he made that afternoon did he discuss the volume of business with his customers. Nor did any of the customers raise the subject with him.

As promised, Joey made a few telephone calls to discuss the problem with his superiors.

At one-thirty in the afternoon on that same Monday Laura pulled her Nisan Altima into the parking lot of the Double Tree Hotel adjacent to the local airport. She hurriedly entered the lobby of the hotel and headed straight for the first-floor restaurant. Ross was already there, seated at a table near a window.

As she placed her purse on the table and took a seat she began, "Sorry I'm late. That damn construction traffic drives me nuts. I swear these guys do a half-ass job on purpose so they can come back the next year and make some more money."

"I don't know about that, but there's no point in getting all bent out of shape about something you can't do anything about. Just have a drink of something and settle down. Should I order you the usual?" Ross remarked in a rather fatherly voice.

"That would be just fine, thank you." Laura said in a more calm voice.

Ross signaled to the waitress and ordered a martini made with Bombay Gin for Laura and a Gin and Tonic for himself. After the waitress had taken the order and left the table, Ross turned to Laura:

"You seem a bit more upset than just being steamed over the traffic. What else is bothering you?"

"As usual, you're right Ross. I've got a really major problem. The IRS is after Tony and me and they want a ton of money from us. And, of course, we don't have the money."

"Tony's met with the agents and his lawyer and they claim we had more income than was reported on our tax returns. They asked about gambling income, so Tony asked me about gambling. I denied it, of course." Laura paused to hear Ross' response.

"Doesn't sound good my dear. I can understand why you're upset. But it's not the end of the world. I'm sure something can be worked out." Ross tried to reassure Laura.

Laura responded, "God I hope you're right. But how the hell can I possibly get out of this mess?"

"How about if I give you money to pay the tax guys to go away?"

"Don't be ridiculous. I'm talking about $20,000. What do I do, go home to Tony and say, oh look honey, I found a bunch of money, or my fairy godmother left this wad of money under my pillow?"

Laura went on: "If somehow my gambling becomes known this whole house of cards will come tumbling down. First, Tony hates gambling. Second I would have to own up to where the money to gamble with came from. Third, that's the end of my comfortable life. This isn't a minor incident, my friend; I'm in deep shit!"

Just then the waitress returned with the drinks that had been ordered, and asked if they were ready to order.

Laura said, "I'm really not hungry," but Ross insisted that she needed to eat something.

"Alright, do you have the half a melon with chicken salad?" she asked.

The waitress answered that her requested lunch plate was always on the menu.

Ross said that he would have a Reuben sandwich, but to hold the fries. He also requested refills for their drinks.

Ross resumed the conversation: "Look, you don't have to be concerned about Tony finding out about the gambling. I've made arrangements with the casino. You're gambling on my account so any government forms that must be issued are issued in my name and Social Security Number. If need be, any gambling winnings show up on my tax return. Therefore, the feds didn't get on your case because of gambling."

"Are you sure about that?" Laura asked.

"Absolutely! I've dropped enough cash over there to be sure my wishes are met."

Ross went on: "So the extra income, if there is any, will have to be explained by Tony. Whatever happens, you just plead ignorance and you will be okay." There's a thing in the tax law called "Innocent Spouse" that relieves one of the persons on a joint tax return of any liability if it can be shown that the person did not know or had no reason to know the tax return was incorrect."

The waitress returned with their orders. While Ross savored his sandwich Laura just picked at her meal. The two exchanged some meaningless small talk while they finished eating their lunches.

Upon completing the meal Ross gave the waitress the money to pay the tab, and then spoke to Laura:

"Shall we retire to our room for our weekly exercise session?"

"I hate to do this Ross, but I have to beg off today. This income tax things has me too upset."

"Don't do this to me. I wait all week for our get together. Besides, a roll in the hay will relax you and take your mind off of things." Ross pleaded.

But Laura held her ground. Her mind was made up and no amount of coaxing by Ross could make her change her thinking. She told Ross that she would call him in a few days, and that by then she would have had time to get her head straightened out. She ended her plea by asking Ross to not be angry with her.

Ross only smiled and caressed her hand softly. "I'll be sitting by the phone waiting."

The two then left the restaurant and went their separate ways.

As she maneuvered through the traffic on the way back to her home the same question kept rolling through her mind: 'How the hell am I going to get out of this mess?"

u

Two weeks passed and Tony had not heard anything further regarding his tax problem: No calls from his attorney and no mail from the government. Then one morning while with a customer, Tony's cell phone sounded; it was his boss on the other end of the call.

"Tony, it's Joey, how are you doing this morning?" His boss said in a rather pleasant voice.

"Not too bad, thanks, how about you? I'm with a customer right now, can I call you back?"

His boss said, "sure Tony, but don't take too long."

After finishing his business Tony returned to his car and immediately dialed his boss' number. After a few rings the familiar "Yeah" came over the phone.

"I got back to you as soon as I could. What's up?"

Joey began, "well my friend, you're in luck. The guys up the line are going to foot the tax bill for you, all 20 G's of it. How do like that?"

"Unbelievable! But what's the catch? Am I going to have to pay it back?"

"No man, you're home free. All you have to do is agree to pay the money to the feds and tell them to take a walk. This is a real break my friend."

Joey continued on, "we think one of our lawyers needs to talk with your guy though. What's his name and phone number?"

"Hang on a second" Tony said while reaching for his address book. "Here it is" he went on, "Donald Roberts, Jr. 555-1234; that's a 809 area code."

Joey concluded the conversation with, "just hang loose until you get a call from this guy Roberts."

Just two days later Tony received a call from Don Roberts informing Tony that a meeting with the IRS had been arranged for one in the afternoon on the following Monday. His attorney asked, and Tony confirmed, that he was ready to pay the tax assessment.

u

At the appointed hour Tony arrived at the office of his attorney. Agents Jim Madison and Jack Adams were already there. The two parties to the tax dispute casually acknowledged each other. Shortly thereafter those three and attorney Roberts took seats in the conference room. Attorney Roberts was the first to speak.

"Good morning gentlemen. With your agreement I am again going to be recording our conversation."

Both agents indicated that they had no objection to the recording of the proceedings.

"As you know from our phone conversation, gentlemen, my client has decided to pay the assessment you have proposed. Do you have with you the documents needed to bring this matter to a close?" Roberts asked.

Agent Adams responded, "yes we have all the necessary paperwork prepared, and we are pleased that Mr. D'Angelo has agreed to make payment. However, before we take the next step, I would like to inform your client of some of the ramifications of his actions."

"Mr. D'Angelo, and I'm using round numbers here, the Government has issued you a bill for some $20,000. That figure includes what is defined as an Accuracy Penalty. One of the reasons for issuing such a penalty is a substantial understatement of the income tax. After reducing the amount of the proposed settlement amount by the penalty component of the liability, it appears that the understatement was in the area of $17,000, and that is certainly substantial."

Agent Jim Madison spoke next. "Again, by rough calculation, a tax understatement of that amount would suggest that as much as $70,000 of taxable income was not reported on the return you filed. Jack described earlier the assessment of a 20 percent accuracy penalty. However, when the amount of unreported income rises to the level that we have in this case we may be moving toward a fraud penalty. That penalty is 75 percent. And of course, fraud against the United States Government is a criminal offense."

"Now we can't just assess a fraud penalty, we have to go to court for that. The burden of proof then shifts to the Service. In court, of course, you would be under oath, and not just be involved in a conversation like we are having here this morning."

"If we determine that it is appropriate to do so, we would then refer this matter to our criminal investigation division."

Tony just sat there with a stunned look on his face.

Attorney Roberts spoke up, "Hold on a minute. The fact that my client may have under reported some income does not immediately cause him to become a felon. He may have used bad judgment, or made a serious error, but that does not make him a criminal. There might well be a plausible explanation as to the source of the money."

"Perhaps he borrowed money from someone. In that case it wouldn't have to be reported on his tax return. Or maybe he hit the lottery and didn't realize it was taxable.

Maybe the person who prepared his tax return made a mistake. I think it's a bit premature to be talking about criminal investigations."

Agent Adams responded, "You're right Mr. Roberts. Those are all possibilities, and maybe the cow really did jump over the moon. We are not talking about failing to report the $100 won at the local church bingo game, we are discussing serious money! History has shown our investigators that amounts of this magnitude often come from illegal activities."

"That may be, but often isn't automatically always. I would like to suggest that we take a break at this time."

The two agents went out to get some fresh air while Tony and his attorney retired to Mr. Roberts' private office.

"Well Tony, what do you have to say?"

"You were right earlier when you suggested that these guys are after something bigger than the 20 G's they want from me. I had the money they're talking about. But I'm in a bind to not let the cat out of the bag."

"Look Tony, if I'm going to be of any help to you I need to know the whole story."

u

Earlier that same morning Laura had telephoned her friend Caroline.

After entering the numbers on her phone, Laura sat back with a cup of coffee in one hand and the cell phone in the other. After a few rings an answering machine began spewing its message. We're not hear right . . . Then a voice cut in: "Hi, wait until this goofy message quits." Laura heard.

"Okay, now that the goofy message is over. Why'd you call?"

Laura explained. "I've got a big problem I need to talk to you about it. How about lunch today?"

"Problem? Not you of all people, so let me have it," Caroline said.

"I can't because I don't feel comfortable discussing it over the phone. I really need you to help me, can we do lunch today?"

"Let me think a minute," Caroline said, followed by, "yeah, I can make it. How does 11:30 sound?"

Laura said, with relief in her voice, "great, and here's another surprise for you. I'll meet you at Denny's."

"Dennys? You have to be kidding me. The way you live I didn't think you even knew Denny's existed. But that sounds great to me. See you at 11:30," Caroline said and then ended the call.

Laura immediately began getting ready for her luncheon meeting with Caroline. All the remainder of the morning

Laura kept running different scenarios of the best way to explain to her friend what has been going on and, more importantly, why it has been going on for so long.

She was aware of the fact that Caroline couldn't possibly offer her a solution to her dilemma, but Laura was aching to talk to and share her problem with some one. Ross had given her some comfort during their recent conversation, but she needed more than comfort. She needed to release some of the pressure she was feeling, and just talking about it gave the promise of some breathing room.

u

The meeting between the IRS agents, Tony and his lawyer resumed after a break of some 30 minutes.

Agent Adams began the session, "just before we took our break we were talking about possible sources of the income that seems to not have been included in Mr. D'Angelo's tax return. I would like to go back to that topic."

"One of the things mentioned was winning the lottery, a form of gambling. We briefly asked about gambling during our first meeting, and I would like to go back to that line of thought. When we raised that subject earlier you denied any gambling on your part, as I recall. Is that correct Mr. D'Angelo?"

Tony said he didn't think the question was answered at that time.

Agent Madison then spoke up. "You are aware of the fact Mr. D'Angelo that gambling is not illegal, per se. One may play the horses at the track or at an off-track betting parlor. One may also gamble at a casino of, course."

"Yeah, I know all that, but the answer is no, I don't gamble."

Jack Adams pursued the issue. "That's interesting. In connection with this investigation we had some of our people visit the locations operated by your customers. It turns out that almost all of them have what we call slot machines in them. I'm sure you are aware of that fact."

Tony replied, "yeah, I know about the machines, but they're just there for amusement, as far as I know."

"Then you haven't been paying attention, Tony. Our people also played some of the machines and in more than one case they walked out with more money than they had when they started playing the machines. That means those machines are gambling devices, doesn't it?"

"Yes, I suppose it does, but how does that effect me? I'm not playing the machines."

"Well we aren't sure that it does, Mr. D'Angelo. That's what we are trying to determine. It seems we have a series of businesses that are conducting illegal gambling activity. All of those businesses are customers of yours. And you apparently failed to report a substantial amount of money on your income tax return. Finally, you haven't revealed where it is the unreported income came from. It would seem to be logical to assume that the illegal gambling and the unaccounted for source of the extra income might be related in some way, wouldn't you think?"

Attorney Roberts interjected, "you guys seem to love to deal in suppositions and innuendo don't you? My client sells beverages to his customers. He does not tell them what they may or may not do within the walls of their establishments."

"You are stretching a good deal in reaching the conclusion, or should I say delusion you have reached. Let's assume that the spouses of some of his customers are having extramarital affairs. Does that lead one to the conclusion that it is my client who is engaging in those activities?"

"Further, although I am not an expert on the tax code, I feel quite certain that nothing contained therein requires a taxpayer to disclose the sources of income upon which he is paying taxes."

"I think this meeting has come to an end. My client will not be signing any agreement this morning. Thank you for your time," Attorney Roberts concluded.

The two agents gathered up their paperwork and left the room.

Tony and Don Roberts sat for a few moments just looking at one another.

"Well, Tony, care to tell me anything?"

"Not yet. I have to check with someone first."

"Tony, you're running up a bill to the tune of $250 an hour and so far all I've been able to do for you is buy time. I certainly like earning the money, but doing some good for my clients is important to me as well. If you aren't willing to cooperate with me you might want to consider engaging the services of another lawyer. Give it some thought."

'No way, Don, no way. I'm just afraid of making a serious mistake. Believe me, I'll come around as soon as possible. Just give me a few more days."

Early that afternoon Tony called his boss to relay the events that had taken place that morning.

After the call had been answered Tony began, "Joey, things are getting out of hand with these IRS guys. We had a long meeting this morning with the idea that I would just give them the money and that would be the end of it. But that didn't happen."

"Why not?"

Tony went on, "they say the amount of money that I didn't report was substantial enough that it might indicate some fraudulent activity. They said that if that were the case we would end up in court, not to mention the fact that they would want an additional $12,750. And the real shit is that fraud moves the case to the criminal division."

"So what did you tell them?"

"My lawyer wouldn't let me say anything. He just told them he thought they were on a fishing expedition and that we would be back in touch with them. Joey, my lawyer wants to know what's going on, but so far I haven't revealed anything to him. What the hell do I do now?"

Tony's boss came back with, "keep doing just what you have been doing. Admit nothing and don't agree to anything. I'm going to have to consult up the line on this thing. I suspect part of the problem might be your mouthpiece. Not every lawyer has experience in matters like this. So don't panic because you are probably being watched."

"I know that too. The feds know about the machines because they have been doing some surveillance in the businesses of my customers."

"They've also been watching you and your wife, Tony. I suspect some of your spending has been stupid and that set them on your trail. When you deal in cash you think you don't leave any tracks. But you do Tony, and any little tip some asshole gives to the feds turns these guys on. They get their jollies by nailing schmucks who think they can out fox them," his boss lectured.

"Hold it right there!" Tony said in a voice he was not accustomed to using when speaking with his boss. He went on, "I might have been born at night my friend, but it wasn't last night."

u

"**I**'ve got some cash on the sidelines. Who knows when things might slow down and the cash flow will peter out. I haven't been spending money like a drunken sailor."

"Oh really?" his boss remarked. "Does that mean you've been asking the big guys to bail you out while you're sitting on a pile of cash? Take my word for it, or ask Lamar's partner, you're better off getting sideways with the Feds than with my boss."

"And we aren't talking just about how you blow your money, we're including your wife in this deal as well. Some woman can go nuts when they're shopping. Ever hear of that Philippine president's wife who had over 300 pairs of shoes in her closet? Shit like that is what can screw up a good thing."

His boss continued, "and it's not unheard of for a guy to have a wife who is an alcoholic or who is addicted to drugs or gambling. From what I've heard those dames are very good at hiding their activities. Then one day the guy catches on, but it's too late; by then the broad has blown the whole nest egg. Are you sure you're on top of the spending habits of your wife, what's her name, Laura?"

"Yeah, her name is Laura. I'll have some serious discussion with her, but I think you are out in left field on this one. When will I hear from you?"

Joey said that he wasn't sure, but that it wouldn't take too long to figure out what had to be done.

The phone call was over.

Precisely at 11:30 AM Caroline and Laura met one another at the entrance to the Denny's restaurant mid-way between their two homes. Caroline was the first to speak:

"Laura, you don't look like yourself this morning. Where's the big smile and bounce in your step?"

Laura responded, "yeah, I know I look like crap, but believe me I feel even worse. I haven't been getting much sleep lately."

"Up playing games with Tony all night?"

"I wish. No kiddo, I've got some really serious stuff to deal with. Let's go sit down and talk."

The hostess, after asking in they preferred smoking or non-smoking, seated the two women near a window. Caroline said she didn't even have to look at the menu because she was dying to have a good old-fashioned Grand Slam breakfast. She asked Laura what she was going to have.

"I'm just going to have a cup of coffee. I'm too upset to even eat."

"Well maybe you'll feel better after we talk. So what's the deal?"

And so Laura began to give Caroline the lay of the land.

"How's this for a list of issues: gambling, infidelity and tax evasion? You heard me right; it's all three of those things and they're all tied together. You'd be losing sleep too if you were in my shoes."

Caroline just sat there looking stunned. She didn't know how to respond.

Laura continued, "Do you recall that a while ago you tried to warn me that gambling could get out of hand if I wasn't careful? And I told you then that you shouldn't worry about it because I had an insurance policy?"

Caroline acknowledged that she did remember that conversation.

"Well I didn't read the fine print in the policy, and I'll get back to that. Anyway the government, the Internal Revenue Service to be exact, has contacted Tony and me. They're asking us to come up with $20,000."

"Tony and his lawyer have met with them and the feds keep asking about gambling. They're saying the money we supposedly didn't report might have come from gambling, and as I've told you, Tony doesn't gamble."

The server arrived at the table and asked for their order. Caroline ordered the Grand Slam, and asked for the eggs to be done over easy. Laura indicated that all she wanted was a cup of coffee. The server filled their cups and left to place the order.

Laura went on: "Now I've been dropping some serious money at the casino, and I haven't been on what you would call a hot streak. You probably don't understand the thinking because you aren't a gambler. You lose some money but you think it's just a fluke. If you stay at it long enough you'll come out the other end. You say to yourself, yeah casinos make money, but that's because the amateurs give up too soon. If I stay at this long enough I'll beat the odds. Besides, how else am I going to get my money back?"

"So I began thinking that maybe my level of gambling was the trigger needed to get the IRS involved. Then I decided to consult my insurance policy."

"Hold it right there. How the hell do you consult an insurance policy?" Caroline cut in.

Laura went on, "that's where part two of this mess comes in. My insurance policy is a guy I got involved with at the Shoe. It started with a casual conversation over a few drinks in one of the casino lounges and just escalated from there."

"This guy, his name is Ross, set me up with a deal where I had an almost unlimited line of credit for gambling. Believe me, it's heaven to be able to gamble and not sweat out whether your winning or not."

The server returned with Caroline's order and refilled the coffee cups.

Again, Caroline cut in: "Why would some guy do that? I don't believe in Santa Claus anymore. So what's the hook?"

Caroline was now only picking at her food, having become totally engrossed in what her friend was revealing to her.

"Simple, I sleep with him once a week," Laura blurted out.

"Holy shit!" was all that Caroline could say.

"Holy or not, it's shit alright. But it gets worse. After talking to Ross I decided to do some investigating on my own. Ross told me that my gambling was on him so there would be no record of my gambling. I checked with the casino and it turns out that my Rossie boy was lying. I've been gambling on my own account and Ross is just guaranteeing my credit."

"Go ahead and eat, your food's getting cold. There's no use in both of us going down the tubes over this."

"I'm at my wits end over this."

"All most unbelievable. I can understand the reason someone would find you to be a tempting sleeping partner, but I don't know how you fell into this mess. What the hell were you thinking?"

Laura responded, "obviously I wasn't thinking or I wouldn't be here telling you this, would I? But the thinking now has to be focused on what I do about this mess."

Caroline offered the following, "first, of course, you have to stop the gambling. You should know by now that you can't win yourself out of that part of the problem. Next you have to tell this guy Ross to take a walk."

"Then you have to level with Tony about the gambling. I don't think you have to mention the insurance policy part of it at this time, but you have to let him know how heavily you have been involved. As I understand it, after talking with some other friends, the IRS will set up a payment plan for you, so maybe you can work it out with the government."

"Thanks Caroline. I feel a little better just being able to talk to someone about this disaster. Let me pick up the check for lunch."

"No way, you need all the dough you can get your hands on." Caroline said as she put a few dollars for a tip on the table and picked up the luncheon check.

After leaving the meeting with Tony and his attorney, agents Adams and Madison returned to their office.

"Well, what's next?" Adams began. "We don't seem to have convinced this guy that he's in deep shit."

Madison responded to the question. "We just have to apply a little more pressure. You can tell by his body language that he's already feeling the heat. If he is gambling you can bet he's not a poker player. His facial expressions read like a book. He'll cave, take my word for it."

"Okay, so what do now? Stronger notices by certified mail, or a notice that we are going to place liens on his house and garnish his wages?"

"No, that won't move this guy. We're going to have to get the local law enforcement guys involved. I've never done it myself, but I'm sure you've heard the old saying, there's more than one way to skin a cat." Having said that Madison picked up the telephone and dialed the number of the district attorney.

After a brief conversation arrangements were made for a meeting between the agents and a representative from the DA's office.

Madison ended the session by offering, "you know Jack, and this organization is sort of like an octopus. We have a lot of tentacles, so if a guy eludes one arm, we catch him with another one. Take my word for it, the game is not over yet."

"I sure hope your right, Jim. This D'Angelo guy is nothing but a smart-ass punk, and I can't wait to see him cry."

u

J oey dialed the telephone number of his boss. As the rings pounded in his ears, thoughts of what to say to his boss raced through his mind. Was he going to take a hit because this loser Tony brought on the heat, he wondered.

His boss answered the phone, "Ross here," he said.

"It's me Joey. I need to talk to you about this D'Angelo thing."

"So talk," his boss responded sharply. "But keep it general. Who knows who might be listening, you get my message?"

"Yeah, I know where you're coming from. The feds have upped the ante. Now they're talking another 12 1/2 G's, plus they're talking about fraud charges."

Ross spoke firmly, "This is not good news. The money's not a big deal, but the fraud business is serious. How the hell did this guy Tony get into the system? Don't you check people out before you bring them in? You know for a few bucks you can learn a shithouse full of information about a person. Ever hear of the internet?"

"Sure I know about the internet and background checks. But a search like that won't tell you whether or not the guy is a jerk. So far Tony has been a straight arrow. He does his job and hasn't thrown any shit in the game. How was I to know this crap would pop up?"

Ross went on, "Well the crap has popped up. How much do you know about what Tony has said to the feds?"

"He swears he hasn't said boo about his job, and hasn't met with the IRS guys except when his lawyer was with him."

"I'll give him credit for that, if it's true. I guess we'll have to get our legal people involved in this. I was hoping we could avoid that, but I guess it can't be that way. I know I told you earlier that our guys would be contacting D'Angelo's lawyer, but now our people will take over the whole deal. Call Tony and tell him about my decision. I'll talk to you later," Ross said and hung up the telephone.

Joey returned his telephone to its place on his desk and leaned back in his chair.

"Man, I don't need this shit. I'm busting my ass to keep things in line, and then some moron goes off the deep end. Whoever said if something can go wrong it will sure knew what the hell he was talking about."

u

Tony and Laura had gone out for dinner one evening that week because Tony suggested they do so. He told Laura that they needed to be alone for a while so they could talk without any interruptions.

During dinner Tony replayed for her what had been discussed in the meeting with the IRS people. He further related some of the conversation he had had with his boss.

Laura, of course, was shaken by what she heard, and wondered what, if anything, she could do.

Tony began, "Laura, this thing is quite serious. That means there is no room for ifs and maybes. Because of the law that I told you about, you know, if you sign, you're in, you must be up front with me. The feds keep going back to the question of gambling. I have to ask you about that again."

Laura looked down at her plate on the table in front of her and said softly, "Honey, I have to confess. I wasn't straight with you the last time you asked me about gambling. I have been going to the casino once in awhile." She was having trouble maintaining eye contact with her husband.

"What's once in awhile?"

"Maybe once a week."

"Once a week! You call that once in awhile? Going on vacation a few times a year is once in a while. Gambling every week isn't once in awhile, that's a habit for Christ sake! How much money have you been blowing on your once in awhile outings? Tony pressed Laura.

"Not very much. I told you before I only play the penny machines. I'm sure it isn't enough to call for an income tax problem."

Tony pressed the issue. "Look, I just told you that the feds are talking about income tax fraud charges. Do you know what that means? I'll tell you what it means; it means huge fines and possible jail time."

"I talked to Joey earlier and he says a new lawyer is being brought in to help deal with this mess. When I meet with the new guy he may want to talk to you too. If he does you can't show up with any of your maybes."

u

"**S**o go over what you have been doing with this gambling thing so you can answer the questions without any guesswork. The feds are just guessing, and I think if we're going to come out of this clean we can't be guessing. Do you understand me?"

Laura reacted to Tony's statement, "please, hold your voice down; people are starting to look at us."

"Absolutely! I've kept a little book that shows just how much I've played. I'm still convinced that it doesn't amount to much. Are you ready to leave yet?"

"No, not really. What other crap's been going on that I don't know about?" Tony responded.

"Other crap? I don't know what your definition of crap is. The only thing I can think of is shopping, and I don't call that crap. Yeah, I probably spend more than I should, but it's not all for me. That nice shirt and tie you're wearing, for example, are part of the crap you're talking about. I also spend money on the kids so they can be comfortable at school with their classmates."

"Okay, okay already. Now who needs to think about voice volume? I'm ready, let's get out of here."

Tony picked up the check, and after a cursory review, put 60 dollars in the folder the server had earlier placed on their table.

The pair left the restaurant and drove home without any further discussion of gambling. In the minds of each, however, the wheels were turning. Laura was desperately trying to think of the answers she might provide during the meeting with the lawyers. Tony's mind continued to evaluate the veracity of the responses his wife had provided to his questions.

U

Early the next morning Laura called her friend Caroline at her home.

After saying hello, Laura began, "Caroline you're my best friend, and I really, really need a favor so please don't say no. I need you to go to the casino with me this morning."

Caroline responded, "look you know casinos and me don't mix, but go on with your story."

"Tony and I went out to dinner last evening. All during the meal he kept badgering me about gambling. That, and the IRS, is all he could talk about. We almost got into a shouting match in the restaurant. I owned up to a little gambling, but I sure didn't tell him the whole story. I have to go the casino to check my account balance."

"So go, you certainly know your way there," Caroline said with little sympathy in her voice.

"No, I can't. I'm afraid to go alone. I need you with me so I will stay away from the machines. I have to do what you told me the other day; I have to give it up, and I need your moral support. Will you go?"

"All right. If you're really serious about this I'll go. Pick me up in about a half hour," Caroline said and ended the call.

Upon arriving at the casino and entering the place the two immediately headed for the VIP office as they had done on their previous visit. Once again the hostess on duty greeted Laura by name and asked what she might do for her.

"I would like a statement of my account please." Laura said.

After typing in a few bits of information, the hostess turned to a printer on the side return of her desk and removed a printout. She handed the document to Laura saying, "Here you are Mrs. D'Angelo. Can I do anything else for you this morning?"

While attempting to maintain her composure, Laura replied that she didn't need anything further at the moment and thanked the hostess. She and Caroline then left the room.

Once the two entered the general area of the casino Laura handed the account statement to Caroline.

u

Caroline looked over the statement briefly and then blurted out, "Oh my God, if I'm reading this thing correctly it says $52,387. I think it says you owe these people that much money. Is that right?"

Laura tried to hold back her tears as she mumbled to Caroline a few words that said; yes she was right.

The pair walked right past Laura's favorite Blazing Sevens slot machines and headed directly to the valet parking area. Once in the car Caroline suggested they stop for a cup of coffee on the way home, and Laura agreed to do so. Laura was also feeling great affection for her friend who was helping her in this great time of need.

As luck would have it, the first place they came upon was the same Burger King that they had visited a few weeks earlier. After entering the place Caroline offered, "As long as we're here I think I'll treat myself to a Whopper with cheese. How about you; it's on me."

"No thanks, I don't feel like eating right now. Just get me a coffee while I go to the ladies room."

The two women sat down at a table and began to talk. "What am I going to do?" Laura began. "This guy Ross I told you about told me that he was taking care of the gambling bill. He said I shouldn't worry, so I wasn't worried. Now I'm scared to death."

Caroline responded, "Worried? I'd be wetting my pants. How the heck did you get in so deep? My Alex doesn't make $52,000 in a year."

"Believe me, it's easy. You just sit at a machine pushing a button and lapping up the free drinks. Once in awhile you put another piece of paper in a slot machine and you just keep going. You get to the point that those pieces of paper aren't even money; they're just tickets to more fun and the chance to hit the jackpot. Remember real gamblers **know** they will come on top."

"And in my case, I didn't give a shit because I thought if I ended up losing my so called insurance policy would take care of things. There was no way I could lose. So what the hell, why not enjoy life? Right?"

"Laura, if you aren't the smartest person I know, you are surely one of the most intelligent people I have ever met. Haven't you ever heard the expression; there is no such thing as a free lunch?"

u

"Yeah, I know that now, but how do I pay for the lunch?"

"I have no idea. If you are asking for a loan from me you are talking to the wrong person. If I had that kind of money I would think I was the richest person in the world. Let's face it a $50,000 lunch is one hell of a lunch."

Laura resumed, "I've squirreled away a little money from what Tony gives me, but no where near that much. Besides there's still the money the government wants from us."

"Maybe you can get the asshole you call Ross to keep his word. Is the guy married? If he his maybe you can threaten to tell his wife about the games he's been playing with you. If she decides to dump his ass I bet she'll burn him for a lot more than 50,000."

"No, he told me he's single,"

"Yeah, sure, and he told you he'd cover the gambling too."

"Look, you can check with the county over the Internet. You can look up marriage and divorce information. Give it a shot. If the guy's married you have a wedge to use. Do it!"

"Thanks. You've given me at least a little hope that there's a way out of this disaster. I even feel a little hungry. Can I have a few of your fries?"

For once that day the two giggled a bit.

u

Around 7:30 one morning of that week two casually dressed men entered Jed's Place. Of the two, one was white and the other an African American. The only other person in the place appeared to be the person behind the bar.

Lamar greeted the customers, "Good morning gents, what can I get you?"

The first of the two customers spoke up, "nothing right now, thanks. We are looking for a Mr. Lamar Bowers."

"That would be me." The man behind the bar responded.

"Are you hear alone?" was the next question from the customer.

"Yep, I can't find anyone else who'll work the early shift."

After placing his badge on the bar showing that he was a county police officer on the bar the customer told Lamar, "then I guess you'll have to lock the place up. We're putting you under arrest."

"Say what?" Lamar began, but was interrupted by one of the agents.

The agent went on, "Before you say anything further I want to read you your rights. You are entitled to any attorney. If you can't afford one the court will provide you with one. Anything you say may and will be used against you. Do you understand?"

"Yeah, Yeah, I understand, but what the hell is this all about?" Lamar said in a voice exhibiting his shock and disbelief.

The agent explained, "you're being charged with conducting an illegal gambling operation."

Lamar protested, "Gambling? What gambling? All I do is run this small-time water hole."

"I'm afraid we can't comment on that Mr. Bowers. All we know is that we have this warrant for your arrest. You'll have to come with us. You may want to bring a little cash with you. Unless you have a rap sheet on file you can probably bail yourself out. So let's hit the road." Lamar heard as an answer to his protest.

The sheriff's officer continued, "I assume you will accompany us without any problems, so I don't see the need for handcuffs, do you Mr. Bowers."

A few days later, after checking his email, Tony found a message from his attorney asking that Tony call him.

Tony immediately placed the call. After announcing himself and the reason for his call, attorney Roberts' receptionist put the call through.

Attorney Roberts came on the line, "Hi Tony, we have a new development. An attorney named Aaron Shefield called me. He says he represents your employer, The Ice-Max Beverage Company. I was told that the company is concerned that your problems with the government might have an adverse effect on its relationship with the IRS. He's asking me to give him copies of all of my paperwork and audio tapes connected with this mess."

"I can't do that, Tony, unless you agree. What do you have to say?"

"I'll do whatever you say Don, but I don't want to lose you as my lawyer. And secondly, I can't afford to be paying another lawyer."

"You don't have to be concerned about either of those things. I told Shefield that I wanted to stay involved and he has no problem with that. Also, he said your employer would take care of the fees."

"So if it's okay with you I will call him and make arrangements to get him the things he's asked for. Then I guess the next step will be for the three of us to meet. Shall I go ahead?"

"Yeah, sure. I've got to get this monkey off my back before I go nuts."

Don Roberts then called attorney Shefield. The two lawyers chatted briefly and arrangements were made to have the audiotapes and documents associated with the investigation delivered to Shefield's office.

Both lawyers agreed that a meeting between the two of them and Mr. D'Angelo was essential before the three of them meet with the IRS agents.

Until that time came there was nothing for Tony and Laura to do but wait, worry and hope for the best.

A week passed and Tony had not heard anything from his lawyers or the government. The pressure within him and the tension between him and Laura continued to build as each day passed with no resolution or hope for one surfaced.

Tony continued to work every day, but he found himself becoming impatient with his customers' questions. That wasn't like Tony whose personality typically mirrored what one thinks of when a salesperson comes to mind: happy go lucky, always smiling, and often a joke to tell. For now at least, that person had disappeared.

Laura too was finding that life had changed. Shopping wasn't as much fun as it once was. And she had kept her word to Caroline and had not been back to the casino. She also began to keep better track of where the money was being spent.

At last Tony received the telephone call he had been longing to answer. The call was from Don Roberts who told Tony that he was to be at Don's office at 10:00 o'clock in the morning the following Monday. He also told Tony to bring all of the paperwork that had been used in preparing his income tax return for 2007, the year under examination.

Don went on to add that Aaron Shefield had called to say he had reviewed the tapes of our meetings with the IRS and that he was ready for a sit-down with the two of us.

Tony thanked Don for his efforts and said he would be there right on time as requested.

He was quite relieved to have received the call, but he continued to harbor some worries, of course. He didn't at all know this guy Shefield. He didn't know if the guy would be looking out for him, or for his boss. And he had no idea what other shit the feds would like to throw into the game.

He realized, however, that he really didn't have any choice in the matter. All he could do was continue to hope and cooperate with his lawyers.

Tony arrived for the meeting with Roberts and Shefield as his attorney had directed him to do during their most recent telephone conversation.

After a brief introduction, the three sat down in Don Roberts's office with Aaron Shefield taking the lead.

"Tony, may I call you Tony?" Aaron began.

"Of course."

"First I need to make it clear to you that my being brought into this matter in no way reflects negatively on Don here. It happens that in addition to being an attorney, I am also a CPA. Tax law is quite complex, such as 6,000 pages of law for example. Not every attorney can be expected to be completely knowledgeable about tax matters."

Aaron went on, "Tony this is, as I'm sure you realize, a very serious matter, and one of great concern to my client. I am here with a dual responsibility; I must represent both you and my client to the best of my ability. I am asking you to take my word for the fact that I will do just that."

"I'm sure you will Mr. Shefield."

"Please Tony, call me Aaron. Let's first look at the facts as we have them.

The service is alleging that you spent more money than was possible based upon the amount of income shown on your tax return. Further, the Service has data to support its position regarding the spending pattern exhibited by you and Mrs. D'Angelo. Ergo, where did the money come from?"

"All I can tell you," Tony began, "is that I only have one job, and you know what that is. I get paid with two checks. I take the checks to the bank; cash them, and then give most of the money to Laura; that's my wife's name."

"You don't pay attention to the amounts?"

"Not really. The numbers wouldn't mean much to me. I was a marketing major in college. All of us business majors had to take two courses in accounting. I barely passed in those courses, and I'm still not sure today how I did that. I look at the stubs and all I see is dollars for this, and deductions for that. It's all Greek to me and as long as I have enough money in my pocket I don't sweat it."

With dismay in his voice Aaron said, "that's is almost too hard to believe, but if that's what it is, that's what it is. It kind of reminds me of the fact that I have a son who is a very successful attorney, but he can't balance his checkbook. His wife has to do it for him, so I guess it can happen."

"Listen to me Tony. This is a question that you must answer in all honesty. Are you certain that all of your income is derived from your employment?" Aaron asked with great emphasis in his voice.

"Absolutely, I swear to it."

"All right, I'll trust you on that one. As you know, the issue of slot machine gambling has been raised. And as Don had already told you, we think the Service is actually pursuing that angle."

"Our position with the Service is going to be, so what? We will, as you already have done, concede that you under reported your income, and we will pay the taxes and fines due. Our goal is to avoid the fraud issues and settle the matter once and for all."

"It has been my experience that it is better if the taxpayer in these cases does not attend the meetings. Therefore, I'm asking you to sign another power of attorney form similar to the one you signed for Don. Any problem with that?"

"Of course not. Hey, I'm delighted that I won't have to meet with those clowns again."

"Hold it my friend. These guys are not clowns. They are capable guys doing their job. They are entitled to your respect, even if you aren't too fond of them."

Sheepishly, Tony said he understood what Aaron had said.

"One more thing Tony, in an attempt to dispel the idea that your employer has any responsibility for the slot machine gambling, I plan to have the owner of the company that employs you attend the next meeting we have with the Service. If you are contacted by anyone regarding this matter your only response is to refer that person to either Don or me. Any further questions?"

"No sir, just point me in the right direction and I'll do as you tell me to do. And thanks for your help."

Then Aaron asked Tony's lawyer Don if he had any questions or anything to add, to which Don said no, he did not.

After Tony signed the power of attorney form, and a brief bit of chitchat, the meeting ended.

Aaron left the office and Don turned to Tony and said, "I think this guy knows his stuff. I feel you can relax a bit."

"Me too," was all Tony could say.

Of course, Laura was beside herself with worry about the tax audit and the possibility that Tony would learn her secret. On Thursday of the same week that Tony had met with Don Roberts and Aaron Shefield Laura decided that she needed to take some action.

Due to the stress of the situation, Laura had not been sleeping well and was rising much earlier than usual. In fact on this particular morning she was out of bed in time to say goodbye to her husband and children as they left the house to go about their daily pursuits.

Immediately after Angela left the house, the last of the family trio to do so, Laura went upstairs to her bedroom. She opened one of the dresser drawers and extracted the manila envelope she kept stashed there, and then went back down to the kitchen.

Laura then placed the envelope on the table and went about pouring herself another cup of coffee. Having done so, Laura sat down at the table and removed the contents of the envelope, and began counting.

The contents consisted of 60 $100 bills, a total of $6,000. This was the money she had told her friend about.

She then put the money in her purse, and went back upstairs to get dressed.

Having done so, as well as combing her hair and putting on a small amount of lipstick, Laura returned to the kitchen. Just as she entered the room the telephone rang. Laura picked up the phone on the third ring.

After seeing the caller-id on the phone Laura began, "Hi Caroline, what's up?"

On the other end of the call Caroline asked if Laura was busy that day. "I'm getting spoiled and feel like going out for lunch, what do you say to that?"

"Geeze I'd love to, but I just can't make it today. I've got a doctor's appointment, and would you believe, a Volley-Moms' meeting. How about tomorrow?" Laura offered.

Caroline expressed her disappointment in Laura's refusal to have lunch with her, and then suggested they have lunch together the following day. Laura agreed, and said she would call Caroline to make arrangements.

Laura shut off her phone and returned to the business at hand.

After skimming through the morning paper, she placed the few dishes from the morning's breakfast in the dishwasher. "No time to do the puzzle this morning," She thought to herself as she picked up her purse containing the $6,000 and headed for the garage.

"There's only one way to get out of this mess," she murmured as she backed out of the driveway and drove off in the direction of the casino.

u

Several days passed with no word from his attorneys. The only reminder of his dilemma, as if Tony needed one, was a letter from the Internal Revenue Service.

Along with the letter was a demand for payment of the taxes due plus some additional interest charges that had been accrued since the time the last notice had been sent to Tony. In addition the envelope contained a Form 9465, Installment Agreement Request, which Tony and Laura could file with the Service.

"How thoughtful of the Government," was Tony's reaction? "I don't run up credit charges and make payments with anyone else, so why the hell would I want to do it with the feds? I guess as the saying "we're from the government and we're hear to help you" goes; Uncle Sam is just looking out for my best interest. How comforting."

As instructed to do by his attorneys, Tony simply ignored the letter. Perhaps ignored is not the correct term to use here. He didn't ignore it as one ignores the junk mail in the mailbox or spam on one's computer. He simply didn't take any action, except to show the notice to Laura.

The two of them discussed the matter at some length. Laura suggested that they enter into an installment agreement to get the monkey off of their backs. She felt that if the monthly payment amount were low enough they would be able to deal with it.

Tony disagreed, although he said he would run the idea past his attorneys.

Finally the call Tony had been waiting for came through. He was informed that a meeting had been arranged and that he would be brought up to date as soon as the meeting was conducted.

Tony was not at all relieved. He had been hoping that the call would be to tell him that the meeting had already taken place, and that the matter had been resolved.

Even though the pressure continued to be felt, both Tony and Laura tried to continue their lives in a normal fashion, with some exceptions in Laura's case.

u

Aaron Shefield and Don Roberts sat down across the table from Jim Madison and Jack Adams in attorney Roberts' conference room. A third person was also present.

Aaron spoke first. "Good morning gentlemen. My name is Aaron Shefield and I have been asked to assist in the representation of Mr. D'Angelo." He then presented the agents with the power of attorney form that Tony had executed at their previous meeting.

Aaron went on. "This gentlemen sitting next to me is Mr. Ross Wells. He is the owner of the company that employs Mr. D'Angelo. I've asked Mr. Wells to join us this morning because I think he may be able to shed some light on what is clearly a misunderstanding on the part of the Service. Do either of you have any objection to having Mr. Wells participate in this discussion?"

Agent Adams replied that he had no objection.

Then Don Roberts asked, "I plan to tape the meeting again. Okay with the two of you?"

"No problem," was the response to his question.

"Good, then let's begin." Aaron said. "As I understand the government's position, there is some question as to whether or not Mr. D'Angelo reported all of his income on his 2007 Income Tax return. Is that correct?"

Agent Adams replied, "Yes, that is the crux of the matter.

"According to the documents I have seen Mr. D'Angelo's Form W-2 that shows income of $46,000 and that is the amount reported as income on his tax return."

Then Mr. Wells spoke up. "Wait a minute. Did you say $46,000?"

"Yes, that's the figure." Aaron answered.

"Well something is wrong there. I know Tony makes more money than that in a year. That amount sounds like the amount he is paid as a base salary. He also is paid a commission."

"If he makes more than that why isn't it shown on his W-2 Form?" Madison inquired.

"I have no idea. I'm the president of the company, not the bookkeeper. All I know is that Mr. D'Angelo receives two checks each payday, one for the base salary and one for the commissions he has earned."

"I hear you saying that Mr. D'Angelo earned more than the $46,000 he reported on his tax return. Is that correct Mr. Wells?" Adams asked.

Wells responded, "I'd have to see the earnings record first, but my best guess would be that he earned considerably more than that."

"That adds another dimension to this inquiry. Now we will have to ask for a payroll audit of your company Mr. Wells. If his not all of his earnings were included on his Form W-2 it's likely that Mr. D'Angelo, and your company as well, haven't paid all of the payroll taxes that are due. Those taxes include Social Security, Medicare and Unemployment taxes." Agent Madison remarked.

"There also are penalties that can be imposed for filing incorrect Payroll tax reports to the government. As I recall the penalty is $50 for each form that was either not filed, or filed with incorrect information."

"Be my guest. I have nothing to hide. But if you will want to talk with the person who prepares the proper payroll tax forms for my company, you better be quick about it. Whoever made this apparent mistake will very soon be history."

Attorney Shefield interjected. "From what I have just heard we have a situation where a taxpayer, relying on forms issued by his employer, made a mistake in the preparation of his tax return. It's seems clear then, that to resolve this whole issue all that need be done is to have Mr. D"Angelo file an amended income tax return and pay what ever that return calls for. Of course we would expect to have the penalties abated. Am I correct in reaching that conclusion?"

"Not quite. We continue to have some questions regarding the legality of the source of the unreported income. Contrary to what many folks believe, we are not just interested in collecting money. The Internal Revenue Service also works closely with other government agencies, such as the FBI and ATF personnel, in their efforts to ferret out illegal activities and unreported cash transactions."

"I'm sure it does. But it should not automatically lead to a witch hunt with my client being the focal point."

"Get serious Mr. Roberts, witch hunts were popular a few hundred years ago in Salem, Mass., but today they are irrelevant.

"That may well be the case."

Attorney Shefield then spoke up. "Gentlemen, you are clearly discussing two separate items. The first of those two is the apparent understatement of income and the underpayment of taxes caused by the income reporting error. The second item is the source of that income."

"Regardless of the source of the income, a correction to the tax return for the year in question must be made. Our position in this matter is as follows: We will make inquiry to Mr. D'Angelo's employer's payroll department to learn the correct amount of compensation paid to him during the Year 2008. We will then prepare an amended tax return and remit the taxes due, if any."

"The second concern you have will have to be examined in another meeting if you wish to pursue that issue further. Will you agree to the actions I have outlined?"

Agent Madison spoke next. "Yes, we will accept your plan of action. The file will remain open, of course, until the amended return has been filed and approved by the Internal Revenue Service. I will discuss the second part of your plan with my supervisor. I will contact you to arrange another meeting if I am directed to do so by my boss."

"Thank you gentlemen. I think we have made significant progress here this morning. Rest assured that no time would be wasted in preparing the amended return we intend to file. Do you have any other questions that we can respond to at this time?" Roberts asked.

"No, nothing else for now."

"Then we will call it a day." Roberts said as he turned off the tape recorder.

After the two IRS agents had left the room, Mr. Shefield asked Don Roberts if he would call Tony and fill him in on what took place at the meeting. Of course Don agreed to do so that very day.

Shefield went on, "I think we made some good progress this morning. I'd say your client is off the hook with regard to any illegal dealings. I'm not so sure that the situation is the same for my client. You can bet, if you'll pardon the expression, that we have not heard the last of this from the government."

"I agree one hundred percent on that score."

Having traveled her now very familiar route, Laura arrived in the valet parking area of the casino. After greeting the parking attendant she walked into the casino and headed straight for the Blazing 777's machines.

A few hours passed during which Laura moved from machine to machine seeking out the one that was hot, all of the time feeding Ben Franklins to the hungry devices.

From time to time she would hit a machine that paid out with some regularity, but then it would cease paying. After losing a bit more money in the machine, Laura would decide that the machine had cooled off and she would move on to the next prospect.

Laura decided she needed to take a break for a while. On her way to the casino snack shop she spotted a group of machines arranged in a circular pattern. In the center of the circle was a bright, flashing neon sign. The sign read, "Progressive Jackpot—$88,545." Having seen the sign Laura said to herself, "what the hell, why not give it a shot and solve my problem all at once."

For the next half hour She steadily fed the machine only to end up down the $100 she had devoted to this effort. She stood up in disgust and resumed her travel to the snack shop.

After lunching on a burger and diet coke Laura took her gambling stake from her purse and counted the money and slot machine tickets she had remaining. She found that she was down $1,500. To put it mildly, Laura felt awfully bad. She just sat there for a few moments contemplating the situation and the possible ramifications if her solution didn't work out as she had hoped it would.

Then she looked up and happened to see a sign with which she was familiar from her many visits to the casino. The sign read "High Limit Area." Laura immediately rose from her seat, and after bussing her tray to the disposal area, she headed straight for the sign.

Playing the machines in the High Limit area is not for the faint of heart. Laura sat down at a four-reel, ten-dollar machine. That meant each play would consume $40 per spin of the wheels. Of course the payouts, should she win, would be much greater than what one would see on the dollar machines.

Once again Laura devoted two hours to the effort needed to solve her problem. And, as was the case before, she would win some, then that machine would "go cold" and she move on to the next one.

During this effort she tried everything: She crossed her fingers, prayed, swore, held her good luck charm in her hand

and kissed the machine, but nothing seemed to work for her. Finally, almost exhausted from the stress, she decided to give in.

She left the casino and waited for the valet parking attendant to bring her car around. Once in the car she started to drive away, but then stopped and parked just before leaving the casino parking lot.

Laura opened her purse and removed what remained of her money. She counted the money twice, and both times came up with the same total; she had only $450 remaining from the $6,000 with which she had left her home just a few short hours ago. Tears came to her eyes as she turned the key in the ignition and began the drive back home.

She made the decision to avoid the expressways and take the long way home. After all, she was in no hurry to get there because she would not be the bearer of good news. All through the drive she kept beating upon herself, "How could I be so stupid? I had a good life, but I wasn't satisfied, so I blew it. What the hell do I do now? Will Tony dump me?"

So intent was she in her remorseful thinking that she nearly caused a serious accident when she almost ran a stop sign. Another motorist had blown his horn that brought Laura back into the real world. After waving an "I'm sorry" to the motorist she continued her journey. Now a new train of thought entered her mind.

"Wow, that was close, I might have been killed. But wait a minute, maybe that wouldn't be all that bad. If I were dead my problems would be gone along with me. I know Tony and I have life insurance policies because I pay the premiums. With the insurance proceeds Tony could pay off my gambling debt, and he would never have to know about that asshole Ross. But how?" was her final thought as she pulled her car into the garage.

u

Mr. Lamar Bowers appeared in court, heard the charges for which he had been arrested, and entered a plea of not guilty.

Due to the fact that Mr. Bowers had no previous run in with the law, bond was set at $5,000. Mr. Bowers made bond and left the county building still dazed by what had taken place.

One day later in that same week IRS agents Madison and Adams called on Lamar in his business establishment.

Adams inquired, "We are looking for a Mr. Lamar Bowers. Is that you?"

Lamar responded that he was indeed the person for whom they were looking.

Mr. Adams showed his credentials to Lamar, and Lamar said, "Oh man I don't need this. I already have more than enough problems to deal with."

'Yeah, we know, and that's why we're here to see you. But this might not be the best time to talk. Perhaps we should come back later in the day so you can have someone relieve you at the bar, like maybe sometime this afternoon?"

"I guess so. Let's see, how about 1:30 this afternoon? It's usually a little slow here around that time."

Agent Madison said, "fine, we'll see you then."

At the agreed to hour, the two agents returned to Jed's Place for the meeting with Lamar. Lamar greeted them, and began with, "I've got a small office in the back. Can we go back there to talk so my customers aren't staring at us?"

"No problem, lead the way."

"Would you like a pop or something?" Lamar asked as they headed to his small office.

"Not right now, thanks."

Once the three were seated around a small table in the office, Jack Adams began the discussion.

"Mr. Bowers, may I call you Lamar?" To which Lamar said, "sure." Bowers continued:

u

"We are aware of the fact that you have been arrested and charged with running an illegal gambling operation. We know that because what you have done is tied into an investigation we have been conducting for some time now."

"Now there are several categories of charges for illegal activities, as you might imagine. Playing poker for money in your basement with some of your buddies is one thing. Running a gambling establishment open to the public is a horse of an entirely different color. In the latter case the charges against you could rise to the level of a felony."

In your state, a gambling related felony can draw punishment of fines up to $20,000 and up to ten years in jail. In other words, this is a big deal."

"Holy shit!" was all Lamar could utter.

"Yeah, we know, and that's why we're here to talk."

He went on: "We have talked with the district attorney and he tells us he may be able to lean a little in your favor in this matter. Have you ever heard of being granted immunity from prosecution, Lamar?"

"Yeah, sure I have. You guys think I'm just some dumb shit just because I'm running this dive. I read the papers and watch the news."

"No, no, Lamar. We don't think that at all. You're just the average guy trying to make a living. You saw a chance to put a little more food on the table and you took the bait."

"You got that part right. So what's the deal now?"

Madison explained: "Here it is, straight up. You agree to testify in the tax evasion case we are pursuing and the D A will have the charges against you reduced to a misdemeanor. A charge like that only carries a small fine, and no jail time. What do you say to that?"

"Well there's no way I can come up with $20,000, and I sure as hell don't want to go to jail, so I guess I have to go along with the program."

"Thank you Lamar. We'll be back in touch in the not too distant future." With that remark by Adams, the agents left Lamar to get back to business.

u

A month had passed since the last meeting between the IRS and Tony's lawyers had taken place. During that time, attorney Shefield had obtained the correct earnings information from Tony's employer. It turned out that the person who had prepared the Forms W-2 had failed to include Tony's earnings from commissions.

Mr. Shefield prepared amended returns, both federal and state and met with Tony and Laura to obtain their signatures. The combined taxes due on the two returns amounted to just over $15,000.

Tony told Mr. Shefield that it would take him a little time to get the money together, but that he would mail the returns as soon as possible.

Shefield said that he understood, but the sooner the returns were filed the better because interest charges were accruing with each passing day.

Tony asked about the fraud charges, and Shefield said he thought the IRS agents had agreed that such an action was probably not required. He added that the issue of the illegal gambling had not yet been resolved.

After they left Mr. Shefield's office Tony expressed to Laura the fact that he felt great relief. He informed her that his boss had told him the company would pick up the tab for the added taxes, so basically they were home free.

Laura was pleased, of course, to hear that news. But deep inside she continued to feel the agony associated with knowing that the casino was expecting her to come up with more than $50,000 to cover her gambling losses. And even more troubling to her was the thought of how she had been unfaithful to Tony in order to feed her addiction to gambling. Given her state of mind, Laura didn't add much to the conversation as they drove home.

Upon arriving home, Tony immediately picked up the phone and dialed the number of his boss. After a few rings Tony heard the customary "Yeah" come over the phone.

Tony began, "Joey, it's me Tony, and I've got some good news. I just left a meeting with one of my lawyers and the tax bite is about $5,000 less than we thought it was going to be. How does that sound?"

"Sounds good to me my friend. If you want to come by my office in a few days I'll have a check for you. But I have to tell you something first. There's been a change in thinking from the people up the line. You'll get the money you need, but it's going to be a loan. The payback will be deducted from your commissions a little at a time until it's paid back."

"I can live with that. After all, it's my taxes, not the company's. My lawyer said the feds were still screwing around with the illegal gambling issue. What do I do about that?"

"You do whatever our lawyer tells you to do. If he says talk, you talk. If he says shut up, you shut up. It's real simple. There's a lot riding on the outcome of this thing, and there probably isn't much room for error, so when in doubt, play dumb."

Tony told Joey he fully understood, and the telephone call was ended.

Tony turned to Laura who had been listening to Tony's side of the call and filled her in on what Joey had said. The two agreed that dealing with the repayment arrangements would be possible without too much strain on their life style.

Of course Laura immediately thought about the effect the repayment plan would have on her gambling activities. She knew she had sworn off gambling, but now that they were getting out from under the income tax issue, she wondered if giving up gambling completely was really necessary.

"But first I'll have to get out from under the bundle the casino expects me to pay," she decided.

The following day Laura took the suggestion that Caroline had offered, and did a bit of research on the Internet. She discovered some facts that she thought she could put to good use.

After logging off the computer Laura picked up the telephone and made a call.

After a few rings, a voice came on the line, "Mr. Wells' office, May I help you?"

Laura replied, "Yes I would like to speak with Mr. Wells."

"And who shall I say is calling?" the person on the other end of the line asked.

"Laura D'Angelo," Laura responded.

After a brief wait Ross came on the line. "Hi Babe, to what do I owe this great pleasure?"

"I'm feeling a little lonely, and I thought we might have lunch together."

Ross spoke enthusiastically, "That sounds good to me. How about tomorrow?"

"Fine, I'll see you at the Hampton Inn at 12:30 tomorrow."

With that the conversation was ended.

Laura began to plan the strategy she would employ when she met with Ross.

Various scenarios of how her next meeting with Ross would unfold wove their way through Laura's mind. She was sure that by the time of the scheduled meeting arrived she would have made the correct choice.

u

Five persons seated themselves around the table in lawyer Shefield's office. Four of them had been at the table before, Aaron Shefield, Donald Roberts, James Madison and John Adams.

Agent Adams introduced the newcomer to the table. "I would like to introduce you to Mr. William Banes, and agent with the Federal Bureau of Investigation. As you know, the IRS is a division of the Treasury Department, and we deal with income tax matters. The FBI is a part of the Justice Department, and it deals with the enforcement of gambling laws, among other things."

"We mentioned in our most recent meeting that we felt that gambling income was a part of the reason for the discrepancies we noted in the tax return filed by your client, Anthony D'Angelo. It became apparent during that meeting that a clerical error seemed to be the cause of Mr. D'Angelo's problem, but the question of illegal gambling remained unresolved. We hope to settle that matter with this meeting."

"Then let's proceed with the discussion and see where it leads us," said Shefiled.

Agent Banes took the lead. "We have interviewed one of the customers of the Ice Max Beverage Company, and he has confirmed some of our suspicions. The witness has agreed to become a state's witness should this matter end up in court."

He went on, "the witness has confirmed the fact that illegal gambling activity was taking place, and that the gambling was facilitated through the use of gaming equipment provided by the Ice Max Beverage Company. Would you care to comment at this time?"

"Yes I would," Shefield began. "For starters, I would ask you to look at these documents. You'll note that they are copies of invoices from the Ice Max Beverage Company made out to some of its customers."

The agents scanned the documents, and agent Adams said, "So?"

Shefield replied, "so if you look at the detail you will see the following: There is a figure that represents gross revenues, followed by a figure titled "Merchant's Commission," followed by a figure that reads "Due Ice Max Beverage Company."

"Yes, I see that."

u

For the first time during the meeting, Don Roberts spoke up, "In other words these receipts are for the rental of amusement equipment that is rented by the merchants on a commission basis. I might add that these receipts are for the rental of devices that play music, what in olden days were called Juke Boxes."

Agent Banes responded, "that may well be the case, Mr. Roberts, but we aren't there to discuss whose records are in the top forty. We are discussing illegal gaming activities."

"So we are, so we are, Roberts replied. "Let me ask you to review another set of documents," he said, and passed a second set of paperwork across the table to the agents.

"You'll notice that the computations on these invoices follow the identical format as those you previously reviewed. The only difference is that these invoices are for the rental of the machines you allege are being used for gambling activities," he stated.

"No Mr. Roberts, we are not alleging that the machines are being used for gambling. As I mentioned before, we have a witness who will testify to that fact."

"You may claim anything you want, but that doesn't turn anything into a fact. But for the minute let's assume that some gambling was taking place with the machines that my client rents to its customers. How would that cause my client to become responsible for the conduct of illegal gambling?"

"It's called guilt by attribution. That is, the illegal action could not have taken place if the party guilty by attribution had not made it possible."

Shefield continued the exchange, "My client has written contracts with all of its rental customers. Those contracts clearly state that the equipment it rents is strictly for amusement purposes. The Ice Max Beverage Company does not condone the use of the equipment for any other purpose."

"But you were aware of the fact that some of the machines were used for gambling and took no action," Banes offered.

"Gentlemen, you seem to be having some difficulty with understanding our position in this matter. Perhaps you need a few minutes to discuss the subject between yourselves. I suggest we take a short break," Shefield offered.

u

On the agreed day, and at the appointed hour, Laura met Ross in the restaurant of the Hampton Inn. Ross rose from the chair in which he had been seated and warmly greeted Laura with a brief hug. The two took their seats, and Ross motioned to the waitperson.

After ordering the usual drinks, Ross spoke, "it's great to see you, and I might add that you look much more cheerful than you did the last time we had lunch together."

"Thank you, and yes, I am feeling much better. And how are things with you?"

"Just fine. Business is going well, and my recent visit to my doctor went well too. And now that I'm here with you things couldn't be better."

"I'm pleased to hear that, but let me ask you another question."

"Of course, ask whatever you want my dear."

Laura asked her question, "How's Doris these days?"

Ross sat back in his chair with a stunned look on his face, and replied, "Doris? Doris who?"

"You know Ross, your wife Doris."

Ross simply sat there not knowing how he should respond. The waitperson arrived with their drinks and asked if they were ready to order. Ross indicated that they had not yet made up their minds, and indicated that he would signal when they were ready to order lunch.

After the waitperson had moved off, Laura broke the silence.

"You've been lying to me, and like a babe in the woods I was buying your bullshit. I can't believe I acted so stupidly. I assume you have been feeding your wife a line of crap as well."

"No I haven't been doing that. My wife and I are married in name only. We haven't lived together as husband and wife for a number of years now. She leads her life, and I lead mine."

u

"How convenient, but the fact of the matter is that you are a married man. Look Ross, I may be a tramp in your eyes, and perhaps based upon my behavior you're right, but I'm not so low that I would knowingly screw up another person's marriage."

"No, I don't think you're a tramp. As a matter of fact I think I may be in love with you. You can't screw up a marriage that doesn't exist."

"How noble of you to say that, Ross. But I can't any longer believe anything you have to say. You lied to me about the gambling losses too. I checked with the casino and I'm on the hook for a ton of money."

"I'll fix that right away."

"Yeah, sure, and I'll believe that as soon as someone proves to me that bears don't take a crap in the woods. We're through, Ross. The next time you will see me is in court when I testify at your divorce hearing. Unless my casino debt is cleared, I plan to have a long talk with Doris."

"If I'm not mistaken, the only reason Doris stays with a scumbag like you is for the comfortable lifestyle she leads. If via a divorce she can get her hands on enough money, she will dump you in a New York minute," Laura paused.

She continued, "Think about it. The casino says I owe it a bit more than $50,000. With your money that amount might be half a year's alimony. The difference is that those

$50,000 payments as alimony will go on, and on, and on. Are you getting my message?"

"Yes, I hear you Laura, but you have this all wrong."

"No Ross, you've got it all wrong, and you have had it wrong from the moment you began lying to me. We are through, and as I said earlier, you won't see me again unless it's in the courtroom. I'll give you just one week to make up your mind and do the right thing."

"Laura, it sounds like you are threatening me."

"No Ross, I'm not threatening you. I think a more accurate term would be negotiating."

"But you only have one bargaining chip, and I have a lot of influence in many places. I can see to it that a person is given a job that pays handsomely. On the other hand, I can see to it that a person loses his job."

"I'm sure you can, but that doesn't change things. You do what you have to do, and I'm doing what I have to do."

"Aren't you going to order lunch?" Laura asked.

"No, I don't feel hungry anymore."

"Too bad, I was hoping I could watch you choking on your food", Laura said as she got up and left the room.

u

The five meeting participants returned to their seats in Aaron Shefiled's conference room.

Shefield began the discussion. "I believe we were discussing who it is that is responsible should illegal gambling take place. Let's pursue that line of thought."

"Here's our position," agent Banes offered. First you rented devices to customers knowing that those devices could be used for gambling purposes. Second, you were aware of the fact that some of your customers were indeed using the devices for gambling activities. And third, you took no corrective action."

"Thank you," Shefield said. "Now let's look at each of the items you have just listed."

'My client rented devices to customers knowing said devices could be used for gambling. Mr. Banes, I can leave this meeting right now and take a trip to the local WalMart. While there I can purchase a deck of playing cards. Now I ask you, does WalMart know whether I am going to have a poker game in my basement, or am I going to have a game of War with my grandson?" Shefield asked.

Shefield went on, "I'll link my response to your second and third points. My client was aware of the fact that gambling was taking place and took no corrective action, as you have stated."

"Let's assume for sake of argument, that I do hold a poker game in my basement. Let's further assume that one of the participants in the game happens to be employed by Walmart. Should that employee then go back to Walmart and expect that company to do something about the gambling? Or should that person report me to the police?" Shefield asked.

None of the agents reacted or replied to Shefield's question.

"My client conducts a business that sells beverages and rents amusement devices to its customers. It is not in the police business. Some of my client's customers might also be selling alcoholic beverages to minors, but it is not the responsibility of my client to do anything about that illegal activity."

"All of us, either in our business or personal lives, have encountered situations where some law might be violated. The majority of those instances are of a minor variety, so we ignore them. Some might be of greater importance, and we are upset by these events. But we look the other way."

"We might not feel proud of our behavior in those cases, but we say, "Hey, I'm not the cops." My client has not, and does not condone illegal activities, whether or not such activities involve the equipment he rents. If and when a law is enacted that requires him to report illegal activities of which he becomes aware I am sure he will comply with those statutes."

"Those are quite elegant statements that you just made regarding your client. Were we in England I feel certain that he would have been knighted by this time."

"No need for sarcasm Mr. Banes. We are trying to deal with this matter in a professional manner," attorney Roberts asserted.

"True, true, and I offer my apologies. Nevertheless, the fact remains that gambling that was not legally sanctioned was taking place."

"No doubt about that, so I suggest you devote your efforts in the future to apprehending the persons responsible for those activities. My client is not one of them," Shefield stated firmly.

Agent Banes did not respond to Shefield's remarks.

Shefield then turned to the two IRS agents.

"Gentlemen, we have informed you that an amended tax return for the year in question has been filed for Mr. D'Angelo. We see no need to file an amended return for my client's company. If it would settle any of your doubts, or answer any further questions you have, you might consider an audit of the tax returns filed for my client's company. Rest assured that the Service would receive complete cooperation from the employees who are employed by my client."

"I see no need to continue to take up your time or ours regarding this matter. So unless you object, this meeting is over," Shefield said as he gathered up the documents on the table in front of him.

"I know I speak for the three of us when I say we appreciate your cooperation and candidness in the discussions we have had. Both agents Adams and Madison will review their findings with their superiors. I will do the same, and if need be, we will be back in touch with you," Agent Banes said.

Tony had stopped for a quick bite to eat in a Wendy's near the business where he had made his last call. After picking up his order and finding a seat he began to eat his meal. Just as he took his first bite his cell phone sounded. He put his sandwich down and tried to swallow what was in his mouth as he answered the call.

"Hey Tony," came the voice over the phone, "it's me Joey and I've got good news."

"Hi Joey. It's good to hear from you. I've been waiting for a call from anyone who could tell me what's going on."

"I guess you haven't heard from your lawyer then. I just got a call from Shefield and he thinks the whole deal is over with. He's not 100 percent sure, of course, but he says he feels very positive about it."

"That's great! I feel like a very, very heavy weight has been lifted from my shoulders. Man, you have no idea what I have been going through. Maybe now I can get back to a normal way of life."

Tony continued, 'I'm still wondering why the feds decided to hit me. I know they were really after the gambling deal, but why me?"

"Well Tony, I may have an answer to that question for you. Do you remember any of the telephone conversation we had some weeks back when we talked about how wives or girlfriends can really screw things up?"

'Yeah, I remember, but so what?"

"You told me then that you and your wife aren't into gambling, right?" Joey went on.

"Guess what? You were wrong, dead wrong. Your wife's a big time player at the Golden Horseshoe Casino. The feds picked up on that and figured it was an angle they could use to apply pressure to you."

For a moment there was nothing but silence between the two. Finally Tony spoke up, "You're bull shitting me, aren't you Joey?"

"I wish I were my friend, but what I said is the gospel truth. She's into the casino for something over 50 G's."

"Joey, I'm in a restaurant and I can't talk now. Can you meet me someplace where we can have a few beers and talk?" Tony whispered into the phone.

"Sure Tony, where at?"

Tony thought for a moment and then said, "There's a place at 115th and Western called the Oasis. Do you know the joint?"

"Yeah, I've been in there a few times. How about at 1:00 o'clock?"

"Fine, that's fine. I'll see you there, and thanks Joey," Tony said as he ended the telephone call.

Joey and Tony spent the remainder of the afternoon sitting at a table in the corner of the Oasis Bar. Joey related everything he knew, while Tony listened. Tony kept asking questions, some of the same ones over and over again. Each of the questions was always answered in the same way, with the truth that Tony did not want to hear and that he did not want to believe.

Some of the questions Tony posed were, "How could I have been so stupid?" "Why didn't I see what was going on?" "What the hell do I do now?"

As the two were preparing to leave, Joey spoke softly to Tony, "Tony I'm not talking to you as your boss now. I'm talking to you as a friend. So listen to me. Right now you're plenty pissed off."

"I can't blame you; I'd be pissed off too. You've had a few beers this afternoon, and that doesn't help matters. Don't do anything stupid. Give yourself a little time to calm down. Think things through before you react. This isn't the end of the world."

Tony thanked Joey for his advice, and the two went their separate ways.

Tony heeded Joey's words. All through the next week he worked hard at maintaining his composure. He worked late into the evening, and left earlier than normal each morning. The objective was to avoid most if not all contact with Laura.

u

One morning of the following week Laura woke around her usual time and came downstairs for the wake-up cup of coffee. Both Nicky and Angela had left for school, but to Laura's surprise, Tony had not yet left for work.

"Good morning, what are you doing home?"

"I have some business I need to take care of here at home before I hit the road. It serious business, and it can't wait any longer."

"It must be really important. You never work from the house, and you never keep your customers waiting. What's the big deal?"

"Before I get to that Laura, let me ask you a question. Will you be going to the Golden Horseshoe today?"

"What the hell is that supposed to mean?" she replied in a defensive manner.

"It means exactly what I said. I said it in English so a smart person like you shouldn't have any difficulty in understanding the question. So I repeat, are you going to the Golden Horseshoe today?"

"No, I am not!"

"I'm surprised at that. Seems to me you've been spending a lot of time there over the past several months. Maybe you have lunch plans instead?"

"Hold it, and hold it, none of what you are asking makes any sense."

"Cut the crap, Laura, you know exactly what I'm talking about. All the time I've been the good soldier, working hard to provide for my family, and letting my wife go about her business without much bitching on my part."

"And all through those times you have been lying and cheating. You're very good at it Laura. You had me completely fooled," Tony raged at Laura.

Laura realized that there was no point in further denials, and sat quite for a moment. Then she took a new approach.

"Yes, I admit that I got caught up in gambling. It was just innocent fun at first, but I just got hooked on the excitement. There isn't much excitement left in our marriage anymore, so I guess I substituted the gambling."

"But that's over now. I've learned my lesson, and I've sworn off the gambling for good"

"You're right, and you actually said something without lying. It's over! I have spoken with Don Roberts and the divorce paperwork is already being prepared. We won't have to deal with any of that irreconcilable differences bullshit; adultery is completely acceptable as a reason for divorce in this state."

"I'm not going to disrupt the kids lives anymore than necessary. I'll be moving out. The divorce order will allow you to stay in this house until Angie finishes high school. Until then I will continue to support this place. Once Angie finishes school the house is to be sold, and you will have to find somewhere else to ply your trade."

Tony turned and headed toward the door. As he reached the door and opened it to leave, Laura called to him, "Tony, what can I say, what will I do?"

Looking back at Laura Tony said, "Well, quoting Clark Gable in the closing scene from the movie Gone With The Wind, frankly my dear, I don't give a damn," Tony said as he closed the door behind him.

Laura just stood still for a moment, almost in a daze from what had just transpired. Then a small smile formed on her face. She moved from where she was and picked up the telephone and quickly dialed a number.

"Good morning, Ross Wells' office. May I help you?"

"I'd like to speak to Mr. Wells."

"The receptionist replied, "May I ask whose calling?"

"Laura D'Angelo," she spoke into the phone.

The receptionist said, "One moment please."

After a short wait, the receptionist came back on the line, and said, "I'm sorry, but Mr. Wells is not accepting any telephone calls."

"Oh how cute", Laura thought to herself. "Apparently macho-man Mr. Wells thinks he can solve all of his problems by simply having his secretary tell certain callers that Mr. Wells is not interested in interacting with them."

"Well, Mr. Wells has another thought coming," she uttered to herself, as she returned the telephone to its place on the cradle. As I am sure I have stated before now, I may have been born at night, but it wasn't last night.

Laura sat down at the kitchen table and opened her laptop computer. She booted the computer and clicked on the "Google" icon. In the search box she typed in the words, "Income Tax Cheats, how to report? Several sites appeared on the computer screen and Laura selected the one she felt was most appropriate for her purposes.

u

Several weeks had passed since agents Jim Madison and John Adams had had their last meeting with Tony D'Angelo's boss with no word having come down from their superiors in the Service. Both agents were frustrated because they believed they had been on the track of a major criminal activity.

On this Tuesday morning, one of the usual routine days for agents not deeply involved in any particular investigation, John and Jim began the day by sorting through their desk inboxes. After wading through a lot of "do this" and "don't do that" memos, John came across a memo from the District Director. The memo simply said, "Please follow up on the attached."

Upon looking at the attached document, John said out loud, "Holy Shit!" followed by "Jim, take at look at this."

The document John handed over to Jim was an Internal Revenue Service Form 211, *Application for Award for Original Information.*

"This is the form that people use when they want to turn someone in for tax cheating with the hope of receiving a reward isn't it?" Jim asked.

John shot back, "Right you are, and look at the names on the form."

Name of Claimant: <u>Laura D'Angelo</u>
Name of Taxpayer Who Committed Violation: <u>Ross Wells</u>

"Okay my friend, but let's cut the bullshit. Do you really think I'm such a dumb shit that I would fall for this crap?" Jim replied.

John responded with, "No man; this must be the real deal. I can hardly believe it myself. Let me look at that form again to be sure I wasn't dreaming when I first read it."

After again reading the Form 211, John said, "To quote the late and famous Jackie Gleason, 'How Sweet It Is!' as he laid the form on his desk.

John continued, "This is so great. We don't have to beg anybody for permission to keep after this guy Wells. As a matter of fact, we have been directed to do so. It's interesting that the D'Angelo dame started the ball rolling. I was under the impression that she and our guy Wells were pretty tight."

"That might have been the situation when we looked at this setup before, but obviously things have changed. We need to find out who dumped whom so we can put the pressure in the right place" Jim replied.

"Unless I'm really, really out in left field, one Laura D'Angelo is the "dumpee", and our old friend Ross Wells is the "dumper". But why? Another woman? Angry spouse? We need to have an answer to that question if we are to hit the right pressure points. Wells eluded us once, and I don't want that to happen twice" John added.

"I think our friend Tony may have skated as well, so maybe we can hang his ass too" Jim enthusiastically added to the plan of attack the two agents were contemplating.

Jim continued on, "No way we blow this one. We've got three targets: Tony Boy, Righteous Rossie, and maybe Tony's wife, the gambler. Especially her since she's the one who filed the Form 211. It's always extra sweet to nail one of these greedy bums who hope to get rich by putting the IRS on the tails of people whom they once considered to be friends. Generally it's an ex-spouse blowing the whistle.

u

As Joey crawled along the so called "expressway" on the way to his office on the Monday morning following Laura's most recent telephone call to Ross Wells his cell phone rang. Using his hands-free device, Joey hit the activate button and said hello. On the other end of the call came the voice of his boss, Ross Wells.

"Joey, are you there?"

"Yeah Ross, I hear you loud and clear" Joey responded.

"Good. Now listen to me and do what I say. You have to shit can that punk Tony What's-his-face, and I mean NOW!" Joey heard over the speakerphone in his car.

Joey reacted, "But why Ross? Tony is a good guy and does a great job for us. He had a little problem with those scum bags that thought they could rip us off, but that wasn't his fault."

Ross shot back, "Well your good guy and his wife are what got the feds on my ass, and I don't need any more of that shit. Need I say more?"

Joey assured his boss that he need not give any further instructions and that he would carry out the instructions he had been given, but he still had a few questions to pose.

Joey began, "Ross, Tony had been with us and provided valuable service to us for several years. The guy's got a couple of school-aged kids to worry about. Further, I think he's going through a divorce. He will feel losing a job now as a major disaster. Can I offer him anything to help soften the blow?"

"Joey, you always seem to amaze me" Ross uttered. He continued, "You should know by now that we do not operate like the Salvation Army. That outfit is in business to help others. We are in the business to help ourselves. We strongly believe in and live by the adage, CHARITY BEGINS AT HOME!"

"Now if you would like to do something for your pal Tony, using your own funds, be my guest. But the house rule is simple: WITH SCREW-UP NUMBER ONE, YOU'RE DONE."

"Ross, sometimes I'm not sure I'm in the right line of work, and now is one of those times. I'll deal with this mess as best I can, and I will follow your direction" Joey said as he ended the call.

Despite his outward appearance and "macho guy" talk, Joey had a heart bigger than himself.

Internal Revenue Services agents Madison and Adams immediately began developing the strategy they would use in following through with the investigation of the Form 211 that had been received by them.

Adams began the planning session, "We already have the corporate tax returns for the company this guy Ross heads up so we can dispense with that step. We will need to pull personal returns for the years that match the corporate returns we have."

"Agreed", Jim Madison added, "And we need to look at the returns of our upstanding citizen Laura D'Angelo as well."

"Why her?" agent Adams inquired.

"Jack, I'm surprised by that question. You've been in this business long enough to know that it is very common for the whistle blower to in some way have been involved with, or short changed by the person being reported. How else would this D'Angelo dame know anything about the taxes of Ross Wells? It's my guess that this broad either got the shaft, or thinks she did, and this is her shot at getting even. In either case, we can use her to get at our original target Ross Wells." Jim replied.

Both agents were well aware of the facts that it seems to be human nature that one wants to get even, at least, or do better than that if that person feels he/she has been victimized by another person. The only drive that appears to surpass that emotion is the drive to save one's own skin. The clever and professional law enforcement agent uses those facts to his/her advantage while involved in an investigation.

When two or more agents are involved with the interrogation process, for example, they will use the "Good Cop Vs Bad Cop" strategy. It works like this:

Bad cop (Jim) to potential witness, "I sure hope you have your papers in order because you are going to be going away for a long time. Usually a first time offender like you can catch a break, but not in this case. Why? Because of how deeply you are involved, and secondly your smart-guy attitude pisses me off. That's why!"

Good cop (John) to potential witness after bad cop leaves the room: "I'm afraid you got caught up in this deal at the wrong time. Jim's wife is giving him a hard time in a divorce deal so he's taking that out on everybody, including you. If you work with me I think I can cool him down a bit. He's really not a bad guy at heart, but I wouldn't take a chance if I were you."

If the ploy works the witness will open up to the good cop and deal with the bad cop in the manner instructed by the good cop. The interpersonal "vibes" that surface in the early stages of the interrogation determines who plays the part of the "bad cop".

The bottom line is that a person who feels threatened would prefer to enlist the help of an ally (the good cop), than stand alone against the foe (the bad cop).

"Got it", said Jack. "Unless we can find some fraud in this deal we are limited to the most recent three years' returns so will start there. Agreed?"

Jim replied, "Fine, let's get going right now. I love the new systems. In the old days I would have to wait weeks sometimes to get files I requested. Now I just hit a few buttons on my cell phone and the requested returns begin printing out in my office. I'm old school, so it took me a little while to buy into the new deal, but now I'm a true believer. How about you Jack?"

"I don't know how you guys did your work in the old days. And I wonder how many tax cheats weren't caught. How the hell could anyone track all of this stuff with a pencil and paper? Some people don't like "BIG BROTHER" watching them, but I love it." Jack added to the discussion, followed by, "So let's get started."

The two agents agreed to share the tasks at hand. Agent Madison was to order transcripts of the personal tax returns of Anthony & Laura D'Angelo, as well as the returns for Ross Wells and his spouse for the same three-year period.

Agent Adams contacted the District Director's office to arrange to have audit letters mailed to both Laura D'Angelo and Ross Wells.

u

Tony picked up his cell phone and began with the usual, "Tony here." It was his boss Joey on the other end of the call who instructed Tony to meet him for lunch at their usual place on that very day. Before Tony had a chance to say anything his boss abruptly ended the call.

Joey put the telephone down and leaned back in his chair. He looked around at his surroundings and thought to himself, "Nice plush office. Decent pay; it's actually better than decent. The freedom to pretty much come and go as I please. It's a great setup, so why do I hate it?"

His thoughts continued, "Because for no good reason that I know of I have to shit can a perfectly good employee. Tony's a guy who I can't recall having ever stepped out of line. And not only is he a solid employee, he's a hell of a nice guy. I think Leo Derocher was right, nice guys do finish last."

Now Joey's conscious entered the discussion. "Well big shot, you can always refuse to do the dirty work. You can just tell your boss, this Wells jerk, to do the dirty deed himself."

"Oh sure", Joey responded to himself, actually uttering the words aloud. He mused further, "and where does that leave me? In the same place as the guy whose ass I would be trying to save. Score? Bad Guys 2, Good guys 0. That sure doesn't make sense or really accomplish much."

Joey then made a decision to put off the final blow to Tony with the hope that some solution to his dilemma might be forthcoming. He would meet with Tony, but describe Tony's layoff as being only temporary. That would ease the blow to Tony, and perhaps lead to a solution.

During this same time frame Tony began to plan his day so that he would be able to meet with Joey and still keep his appointments with his customers. Of course he was still wondering what had precipitated the call from his boss, and was even more concerned with the tone of voice Joey had used during the short telephone call.

An inner voice spoke to Tony: "The phone call was not about a raise Tony. Something not very good is going on, and it is not good news for you. Where did you screw up?"

Tony tried to remember recent events to identify a place or deed where he might have messed up. Nothing came to mind. After the fiasco with the slot machine rigging Tony had become much more diligent in paying attention to details. He also adopted a more callus assessment of his clients' motivations, and therefore accepted nothing at face value. No shortcomings came to mind.

It had been several weeks since the time Laura had filed the Form 211 with the Internal Revenue Service. Laura was a member of the "I want it now!" generation, so she was rather upset that each day's trip to her mailbox ended in another disappointment.

"What the hell are we paying these people for?" she asked herself. Then speaking aloud, even though no one was around to hear her words, she went on: "How am I supposed to live the way I want to live on what good old Tony is paying? Yeah, his money takes care of the kids needs, but what about me? I'm entitled to something after all of the years I gave him, right? And to think that just a short while ago I was feeling bad about having to tell Tony I lost the money. Why should I feel bad about it? He didn't feel bad when he dumped me.

"And then there's that creep Ross. After all of the good times I showed him you would think he'd have some kind of conscious. But, no; all he can come up with is he's not taking calls. Bull shit, he'll take calls when Uncle Sam is on the other end of the line."

She continued her rant, "If it weren't for that asshole I wouldn't have the crap I'm having to deal with. He led me down the garden path to the excitement of the casino and now I'm supposed to just sit around and watch the grass grow. I don't think so!"

"So what do I do? Well first I go to the Shoe and see if Mr. Wonderful actually cut off my line of credit. If he didn't, he will wish he did. If he did, I guess I will have to try to sweet talk my way into a bit of credit. Considering the amount of time I've spent there in the past few months I'm sure someone will go along with giving me at least a minimum line of credit. After that, I'm home free."

Laura went on, "On the other hand, maybe there's another sugar daddy hanging out looking for a little side action. Good old Ross Boy can't be the only guy in town with a little extra mad money. If the guy's going to blow the dough, why not blow it on me? I can't think of a more deserving person than I am."

Laura began to get ready for a trip to the Horseshoe Casino. She was already counting her winnings, and picturing herself gloating as she showed Ross the result of her gambling skills. What a sad piece of crap that guy Ross is, she thought to herself.

Prior to backing the car out of the garage Laura decided to check the day's mail.

The only document she found in the mailbox had a return address of the Internal Revenue Service. Great, she thought as she quickly tore open the envelope to find:

Internal Revenue Service
United States Department of the Treasury
Memphis, TN 37501-1498

Tracking ID: 100118219020
Date of Issue: 12-09-2010

Anthony D'Angelo and Laura D'Angelo
5911 W 55th Street
Bollingbrook, IL 60502-1234

Tax Period: December, 2009
Form 1040

Request For Appointment

Dear Mr. & Mrs. Anthony D'Angelo,

A review of your tax filing for the period noted above has been selected for review by our automated screening system. Items at issue are:

Unreported Income

Please contact us at 1-800-477-1000 some time during the next 30 days to arrange a meeting at which time we will expect you to be prepared to substantiate the figures used in preparing the tax return that is the subject of this examination.

If we are not contacted by you we will schedule the required meeting. You may appoint another person to represent you in this matter by completing Form 2868, Power Of Attorney.

Sincerely Yours,
Becky Sharp

Rebecca Sharp, Director
Audit Division

To herself Laura moaned, "Oh Shit, I really needed this!"

However, upon putting the letter back into the envelope in which it had arrived she came to her senses, saying, "Well to quote a dear friend of mine named Alfred, 'What, me worry?' After all, the first name in the address is Anthony D'Angelo. I'll just let good old Tony deal with this shit. I don't have time for it.

Upon removing her cell phone from her purse Laura pressed "Directory, then Tony's cell phone number, and then punched send with an exaggerated motion.

As she sat in the car stewing over the delay in getting about her business of the day Laura first heard the repetitive ringing, and then the recorded voice: Blah,

Blah, Please leave a message after the tone."

In an animated fashion, Laura left her message: "Guess what Big Shot? The IRS is after your butt. Give them a call at 1-800-477-1000. If you don't call them they will come after your ass. Keep me out of this mess, Jerko. I just signed where you told me to sign".

With that Laura put the phone back in her purse and started the car. As Laura negotiated the familiar route from her home to the casino irritating thoughts related to the IRS letter tugged at her mind, beginning with:

"If you signed the return you are accountable for its content" she recalled from

Tony's lecture every year."

The time-worn adage, ignorance of the law is no excuse, reverberated within her scull.

At last she arrived at her destination and turned the car over to the parking attendant. As Laura entered the casino her gait lacked the effervescent hop that she once had routinely demonstrated.

"The IRS odds are worse than they are here". She thought to herself.

On that same day Ross Wells received a similar communication from the Internal Revenue Service, explaining the reason for his call for Tony's immediate firing.

After completing his second business call of the morning Tony departed the Come Back Inn, a local watering hole frequented by a cadre of regular "shot and a beer" drinkers, and flopped down in the seat of his wheels. Before turning on the ignition Tony keyed in the information needed to bring up a list of calls and messages he had missed while talking with customers earlier that morning.

The first couple of items were obviously from some sales wonk pushing the next investment guaranteed to make Tony a millionaire over night. "If only it was that easy", Tony softly uttered to himself.

He went on, "Most of the time I feel like I did when I was a kid with a paper route. I not only had to deliver the papers in a superior manner, I had to go around and collect money for the delivery. Just like now, most of the customers had an excuse for why they weren't able to pay at this time. Same old bullshit!, just a new genration"

A few more unrecognizable numbers popped up before a notice of a voice-mail message appeared.

Immediately after hitting the appropriate key on his smart-phone Tony saw the identification of the person who left the message; Laura D'Angelo. Tony's hand became to shake uncontrollably, not in fear, but in rage.

Laura's words washed over Tony like lava spewing from a volcano; overpowering, all consuming in their effect. Tony hit the "end" button and just sat back staring through the windshield of his car.

He slumped back in the driver's seat of the car and pondered to himself: "Won't this crap ever stop piling up? Why do I have to get involved with my Ex whose a liar? What bad news awaits me when I meet with Joey today? And then there's the IRS bullshit". Of course, no answers surfaced.

Upon further reflection Tony probed his inner being with an important question: "Why should I be the patsy and take all of the heat and suffer all of the losses from this mess? I know what's been going on, and I know what it is the Feds are after. So what do I do, just bend over and grab my ankles so I can get the shaft? I don't think so!"

Tony began to formulate his strategy: First, meet with Joey. Second, talk with his attorney regarding the IRS crap. Third, begin to network to find a new employer because he knew that once he began to cooperate with the IRS his current job would be history.

Upon entering the casino Laura immediately headed toward the VIP reception area. Putting on the best face possible under the circumstances, Laura enthusiastically greeted the hostess on duty. The response she received was less congenial.

"Hello Laura, what might I do for you ?" asked the hostess, a 20ish college grad no doubt looking for a real career, but making ends meet here for the moment.

Laura began, "As you may know, there has been some change to my casino profile. I'm wondering what my current credit limit is?"

"Let me check", offered the hostess as she brought Laura's profile up on the computer screen to the left of her office desk.

"Oh my" was the hostess' first reaction. "According to what I am seeing here your limit is zero.", she went on. "Let me check again. You know how goofy these computers can be sometimes."

After keying in another request for the credit limit in Laura's name, the message on the computer screen came up with the same result; NO CREDIT APPROVED.

Laura had moved around the hostess' desk and peered at the computer screen, and upon seeing the report, thanked the hostess for her efforts and moved on to the casino floor.

"Screw'm", she thought to herself as she headed for her favorite BLAZING SEVENS one-armed bandits. "I'll show this dump what winning is all about. And when I get my reward from Uncle Sam for reporting the tax-cheat Ross I'll really be on a roll," she valiantly tried to convince herself.

As Laura moved through the casino floor she kept a keen eye out for a person, male of course, that appeared to be unaccompanied by a wife or girl friend. Despite her high level of self-confidence, Laura was well aware of the fact that having a "benefactor" would make life much less stressful for her.

u

After consulting with his attorney, Don Roberts, Tony did as he was advised to do and called the telephone number Laura had given him in her telephone message. Tony left a number for a call back rather than wait for an eternity for a line to open so he could actually speak with a live person. Included in the message was a request that either Agent John Adams or Agent James Madison return his call. It seemed to make some sense to Tony that he deal with persons with whom he had already had some experience, and who apparently thought he had a clean slate.

Quite unexpectedly, Tony received a return call that very afternoon. The call was from John Adams.

"Hello Tony, how's it going", Adams began. "This is John Adams with the Internal Revenue Service returning your call."

Tony, quite taken aback by such a quick response offered, "Man, you guys don't waste much time do you?"

"Well my friend", began Adams. "You recall the old saying, 'We're from the Federal Government and we're here to help you'. What can I do for you?"

"You guys sent us, my soon-to-be ex-wife and me a letter saying you want to meet with us and included a number to call; so I called. So what now?" Tony asked.

"Guess what?", Adams began, "Actually we are more interested in talking with Mrs. D"Angelo. I suspect that might come as good news to you, given the divorce deal and all of the crap that comes with that. I know my friend, I've been through the divorce mill." (Good Cop here?) "So you need to get a hold of her and have her call us to set up an appointment." John finished.

Tony shouted back, "NO WAY MY FRIEND. IF YOU WANT TO MEET WITH THAT SLUT, YOU CALL HER!"

"Easy, easy Tony" came agent Adams' response. "Is her telephone number still the same as it was when last we talked?"

"I don't know and I don't give a shit" is all Tony could muster.

"Okay, Okay, I hear you man. We'll call her. Hang in there my friend" said agent Adams as he ended the call.

Laura's afternoon at the shoe proved to be very run of the mill; win a little, lose a little, win a little, lose a little more. Further, no potential sugar daddy could be located. All in all, Laura thought to herself, "What a bummer!"

Laura chatted briefly with the parking attendant who had retrieved her car for her. "Nice to see you again Laura. Where have you been hiding?" the valet offered.

"Well, let's say I just took a sabbatical, you know, a break to get my head together. My husband, ex-husband before long, threw some real shit in the game. It's taken me a while to right the ship, but now I'm ready to cruise again.

You'll be seeing plenty of me from now on." Laura explained with some bravado in her tone of voice and mannerisms.

"Oh, and by the way, now that I am a free woman I'll be looking for a sport to spend some time with me. Keep your eye peeled for me, okay?" Laura added.

Although she appeared to have sold her story to the car-parker, deep inside she felt the pangs of self-doubt. Not being 150 percent sure of herself was new territory for her, and she wasn't sure of how to play this new game. And to make maters worse, Laura realized that, in fact, it really wasn't a game she was playing. It felt more like a sudden death contest.

As she hopped into her car she tipped the attendant and drove toward the exit.

Despite the constant campaign waged to discourage using a cell phone while driving, Laura went ahead and used her phone to check for missed calls/messages. She nearly went off the road when she listened to a message from one John Adams with the Internal Revenue Service.

Quickly, however, she regained her composure and allowed a slight smile to cross her lips. "This could be good news", Laura thought. The possibility that the call was about the form she had filed when she decided to nail the hide of the skunk to the wall.

"I didn't have a good day at the shoe, but who knows, maybe I hit the jackpot after all." With that thought in mind Laura noticed that the sun was suddenly shining more brightly, and that the traffic was flowing more smoothly. All seemed right with the world.

Laura replayed the message left by the IRS agent to be certain that she had not missed anything upon first listening to it. The details of the message did not reveal the reason for the call, causing Laura to hang on to her rosy version of what prompted the call.

Without losing any time Agent Adams has obtained an order requiring the Horseshoe Casino to provide the agent with the gambling records of both Laura D'Angelo, Anthony D'Angelo and Ross Wells.

With no resistance, the casino complied with the order.

With the arrival of computers and electronic communications it is quite simple for the management of the casinos to keep track of the gambling of its regular players.

The first step is to lure the player into joining a "rewards" plan and have an identification card issued for that player. The sales-pitch is, of course, "the more you gamble, the more rewards will be available to you. Rewards such as free meals, free rooms, and even cash are dangled in front of the player.

Therefore, whenever a gambler gets involved in the action the ID Card is used.

Of course that allows the house to track the action. With an analysis of the various patterns demonstrated by the players being observed, key targets for follow-up are identified. Certainly, during her recent and regular casino outings, Laura D'Angelo was tagged as an important player.

In addition to keeping track of how much money was being wagered, and in what games the player was involved, slots, poker, roulette, etc., the accounting system also keeps track of the source of the funds being wagered. i.e., cash? Credit? Personal Check? Third party guarantee?, etc.

Security cameras strategically hidden throughout the casino allows casino employees to observe who it is that is using a particular club-membership card.

Is one person spending all of the money being wagered, or is the card being passed around among members of a group? The former is much preferred by the casino management.

With enough gambling activity the player will be approached, in person or via email, by a person who introduces him/herself as a casino host/hostess. That person's role in life is to make it as easy as possible for the player to gamble, and lose, of course.

Laura certainly had a host while she was burning through Ross' money, but when her line of credit was cut off she also lost the services of a hostess.

A major loss, as far as Laura was concerned. Laura enjoyed being courted by the casino host.

Agents Adams and James Madison poured over the computer printouts that they had obtained from the casino. The report indicated that Laura D'Angelo was strictly a slot machine player. It further revealed that she had a pattern of starting each session playing the $1.00 machines. Then if the tide was running against her she would back down to 25-cent machines, and then down to Penny Slots.

Once the tide seemed to be turning Laura would work herself back up the denomination table. Occasionally, if she felt like she was on roll, she would venture into the high rollers area and play some of the $5.00 and $10.00 machines.

As one knowledgeable of how casinos operate would expect, the final tally was in favor of the casino.

Other aspects of the report showed that Laura's credit line was, from time to time, restored to a top level of $25,000. And further, the replenishment of the account always was made with a cash deposit. There was no record of who the person was who deposited the cash with the casino.

That fact caught the eye of both Adams and Madison. Who the heck dumps money into a casino while never using a check so that the origin might be traced back to the writer of the check? People in general seem to believe that dealing in cash leaves no footprints. But that is not always the case.

Assume you are an employee of the casino. Assumes further that from time to time a person appears before you and wishes to make a deposit to his casino credit account. And further, this person always presents you with a stack of $100 bills. Might you recall who that person might be, or at least what his appearance was? So much for the absence of a footprints leading back to the source of the funds.

Adams spoke first, "Man this dame sure burned through a hell of a lot of dough. We know what kind of money her husband made, and no way could those earnings support gambling at this level."

"Amen my friend." Madison responded. "I think the source of the added cash is the link between Laura D'Angelo and our so far the elusive Ross Wells.

I'm not much into praying these days, but if it helps to nail this hotshot I'll give it a try."

u

Tony met with Joey at the appointed time and place; the table tucked back in the corner of the restaurant. Joey preferred the location because its off the beaten track lent it an aura of privacy. Frequently topics being discussed were best not overheard by persons not included in the conversation.

Joey welcomed Tony with his customary curtness. To those who did not know Joey, and understood his personality, Joey could come across as being very cold and domineering. Tony, of course, took Joey's mannerism in stride and returned the greeting.

"Well where's the fire?" Tony began.

"Fire, what fire, what the hell are you talking about?" responded Tony's boss.

"Joey", Tony began, "I get a telephone message that says meet with me NOW with no explanation, or even a chance to ask a question as to why the urgency. Naturally I assume some major event has taken place or some serious problem has popped up."

"You're correct, Tony, and that doesn't surprise me. You're one of my best field people; never late, never offering any nonsense excuses, always alert and on the ball. So I am forced to do something that I would surely like to avoid doing, but I can't."

Joey continued, looking for a way to ease the pain he was about to inflict, not only on Tony, but on himself a swell as.

"I'm not a psychologist, and this isn't a shrink session, but I'm trying to find a way to get you to understand the abruptness of my call this morning."

"There are times when a person has to carry out an order with which he does not agree. In such a situation the person becomes angry. When said person is in the act of carrying out the directive coming down from higher-ups, the anger shows itself in the confrontation."

"If the other party to the discussion appears to be angered; all the better for the one delivering the message. Well Tony, that's me, the bearer of bad news. I have mixed feelings: Do I hope you express anger, or do I hope you understand that I am, as claimed by many others in this situation, only doing what I've been ordered to do?"

"Yea I'm hot, and I think I have a right to be mad. So let's quit beating around the bush. What the hell is up?" Tony said firmly.

"As you wish my friend. I've got orders to dump you, now." Joey blurted out.

Oh man, I hope I didn't hear that right, Tony thought. I really don't need this crap. The divorce bullshit is enough to deal with.

"Joey, look me in the eye and tell me I didn't hear you correctly when you said you were letting me go." Tony said softly.

"I can't do that Tony. You heard me right. Word came down just this morning. No reason, no time period, just let him go, now, period!" Joey chose his tone of voice carefully in an attempt at softening the blow.

He continued on before Tony had a chance to react. "I'm trying to make arrangements to buy some time, or to have this simply be a move from full to part-time. I should know in the next few days, but for now you are off the payroll."

"To tell you the truth Joey, I've been expecting this. As a matter of fact, I'm somewhat surprised that this deal didn't go down earlier. And let me guess who the assassin is, Ross Wells. Am I right?" Tony inquired.

Joey replied that Tony was correct in his guess as to who was behind this action.

"Well Joey, you can tell your boss for me that he hasn't seen or heard the last of me. I played the good soldier and kept my mouth shut when those IRS guys were digging around. Looks like that was a mistake on my part. But now I have no reason to protect anyone, and its time for me to begin worrying about my own welfare. And that's exactly what I plan to do." Tony offered as he rose from the table.

Tony extended his hand to shake with Joey and reassured Joey that he held no ill feelings toward him. After the two shook hands warmly, Tony walked away.

u

Laura had returned the call from the IRS agent and had made arrangements to meet with them in the offices of the District Director, which was in the suburban town adjacent to where Laura lived.

Unlike most persons entering into such a meeting, Laura did not feel any apprehensions. After all, she thought to herself, I may be hitting the jackpot.

The majority of people showing up for a meeting with the "Feds" have sweaty palms as they expect the worst, but hold out hope for a reasonable resolution to whatever the issue might be. Those persons also find appearing in the "enemy's backyard" to be quite intimidating.

Laura approached the reception desk, stated her name and the reason for her being there. She was told to have a seat and that someone would be with her shortly.

After about ten minutes, a time-span that seemed and eternity to Laura, Agent Adams came out from an inner office and greeted her.

"Good morning Mrs. D'Angelo. Thank you for coming in. Won't you accompany me to our conference room?" The agent said in a friendly manner.

The two entered one of the conference rooms in the office complex where Agent Madison waited. As Laura entered the room Agent Madison rose from his seat, extended his hand toward Laura and introduced himself to her. He then asked if Laura would like a cup of coffee or a soft drink of some kind. Laura declined the offer.

"You'll recall, Mrs. D'Angelo, that a short while ago you received a letter concerning the return you and your husband filed for the year 2009. I have a copy of that return in this file folder." Agent Madison explained.

Laura tensed up and sat upright in her chair. "Is that why you had me come in to meet with you? Why didn't you say so when I called to arrange this meeting?

I don't know anything about that return. I just signed where my husband told me to sign, so you will have to have him answer your questions." Laura said as she began to get up from her chair.

Agent Adams spoke up, "Please stay seated Mrs. D'Angelo. I'm sure we can discuss this matter in a professional manner. You see, Mrs. D'Angelo your signing the return makes you fully responsible for its content. We have already had a talk with Mr. D'Angelo.

Laura sat back with a sigh and asked the agents the reason for their wanting to speak with her.

Adams continued, "May I call you Laura?" he asked.

Replied Laura, "No you may not call me Laura. This is not a social visit, so let's get started. Why did you drag me down here?"

"As you wish MRS. D'ANGELO" Adams went on. "Are you aware, Mrs. D'Angelo that gambling winnings constitute taxable income?"

Laura responded that she was not aware of that because she didn't know anything about taxes, and repeated again that all she did was sign where told to do so.

Let me read you a statement that appears at the bottom of the Form 1040 that you and your husband signed." Adams went on: "*Under penalty of perjury, I declare that I have examined this return and accompanying schedules and statements, and to the best of my knowledge and belief, they are true, correct, and complete.*"

He continued presenting the reason for the meeting which was beginning to grow quite intimidating for Laura.

"The age-old adage that ignorance of the law is no excuse is particularly apt when looking at United States Government's Income Tax Code.

The reasons you are here today are that 1, you had gambling winnings in the Year 2009, and 2, none of those winnings is included in the tax return you filed for that year. So you see, it's a simple matter that you had income that was not reported as the law requires." and with that, Adams sat back in his chair and looked for a reaction from Laura.

"How do you know I had gambling winnings in that year?" she meekly asked.

Madison became involved in the conversation with, "Mrs. D'Angelo you are not a country bumpkin. I'm sure you are conversant with the many fascinating operations which computers are capable of performing. So keeping track of the gambling patterns of its regular players is a simple task for casinos. So to answer your question about how we know about your gambling, the answer is, we asked."

u

Laura blurted out, "But I had losses too. In fact I think I lost more than I won."

"Yes you did Laura. But that doesn't mitigate the fact that you and your husband understated your gross income on the tax return you filed for the Year 2009. As a matter of fact, using IRS Guidelines as a rule, the facts seem to support a charge of a substantial understatement of income. The law calls for an automatic 20 percent fine for that offense. Care to comment on this situation? Madison asked.

"I don't know what to say." Laura began. She went on in a much more subdued tone of voice, "Have you discussed this with my husband?"

'Yes, of course we have. We didn't, however, discuss with Mr. D'Angelo the extent of your gaming activities. Does he know how much you gamble?" Madison inquired.

"I think he has a good idea of my addiction. That's a big part of the reason we are getting a divorce." she responded.

Agent Adams, returned to the conversation, "You just used the term 'addiction'

Mrs. D'Angelo. Do you really think you are hooked on gambling?"

"Well, before today I would have said no, but now I'm not so sure. Getting a divorce isn't fun. But perhaps having to pay a major fine, or even spending some time behind bars brings the answer to that question much more into focus. What can I do to soften the blow?" Laura pleaded.

The back of Laura's mind was churning the problem over and over, trying to think of a way out of the mess in which she found herself. This Adams guy seems to be somewhat sympathetic. Maybe I can make him a deal of some kind. If they think I'm an addict of some sort they will probably be willing to give me a break. But what do I have to offer? she wondered.

"Mrs. D'Angelo" Jim Madison began, "you gambled a good deal of money during the Year 2009, and until fairly recently you have continued that pattern. We know that some of the money you gambled was money you won previously, but over all you lost far more than you won. Which, of course, leads to the question, from where or whom did you get the money?"

He added, "You've stated that your husband was unaware of your gambling, so we can rule him out as a source of the funds. You are not employed and that eliminates that as the well from which the money flowed. Additionally, we do not believe in Santa Claus or the tooth fairy."

"Would you care to fill in the missing link to this problem? Doing so might be of some benefit to you." Madison said as he sat back in his chair and stared at Laura.

"I'm not sure the two of you are being straight with me", Laura began. "You seem to know a great deal about this whole mess: The fact that I gambled, the amount of my winnings and the amount of my losses. Am I supposed to believe you don't know the source of the gambling stake?" she asked.

"You're almost correct, but what we have is an idea and not a fact. Your confirming our suspicions would be helpful to us, and would likely be of benefit to you as we work through this investigation." Adams told Laura.

After a few minutes of silence Laura spoke up. "I guess I don't have much of a choice. Besides Ross Wells, the guy who put up the money, is a real creep, and I can't think of any way that I should be doing him any favors. Does that answer your question?"

Madison responded, "Yes it does Mrs. D'Angelo. Would you be willing to testify to that in a court of law if it comes to that?"

'Yes I will testify if required to do so. Now what happens?" she asked.

"Well for now, Mrs. D'Angelo, you can go home and wait for us to be back in touch with you. Your cooperation this morning may prove to helpful to us in another investigation. If that comes to pass we may be able to offer some relief to you in regard to your personal tax return for the Year 2009. Unless you have any questions this morning's meeting is concluded. Again, thank you for coming in and for working with us." and with that Laura arose and left the room.

"Bingo" was the first thing out of Adams' mouth once Laura was out of the room. "Just as we surmised, Mrs. D'Angelo is the "dumpee" and she seems to be quite warm to the idea of nailing Mr. Ross' hide to the barn door. That doesn't mean she's home free, but her problems will only surface again after we have dealt with one Ross Wells."

Adams concluded with, "It's been a great morning. Let's get some lunch. I'm buying."

For several days after meeting with Joey, and learning of the decision to put him in the unemployment line, Tony just sat around in the furnished studio apartment he rented after walking out of his marriage to Laura. Actually it was more of a motel room than an apartment, but what really mattered was that it had all of the amenities Tony needed: A bed, a bar, a refrigerator and a TV set.

As Tony had mentioned to Joey when the income tax issue first appeared, Tony had some cash stashed for a rainy day, and as far as Tony was concerned, this was more like a thunder storm than a rainy day.

Across the street from the building in which Tony was a temporary resident, he hoped, was a neighborhood tavern. While sitting at the bar there one evening he struck up a conversation with one of the tavern's regulars. During the course of the small talk Tony mentioned that he did sales work, but at the present time he was unemployed.

Without naming any names Tony lambasted his former employer for giving him the shaft.

After listening for a while Frank, the guy who Tony was commiserating with at the bar, offered some advice.

"Well my friend", he began, "There's a way you can get a little revenge at least."

"Oh really? How do I do that?, Tony inquired.

Frank seemed to be well versed in the subject. "You simply go down and apply for unemployment. When you are approved two things are going to happen, both of them good for you."

"Number One, you will begin to get a weekly payment. And Number Two, your former employer's tax rate is very likely going to skyrocket. That means you end up with more money, and your old employer is going to end up with less money. Is this a great country, or what?" Frank concluded.

After ordering another drink for himself and his conversation partner Tony started, "I don't know. I've heard war stories about what a hassle this unemployment process is. You know, stand in line, bow and scrape to some political appointee, etc, etc. I don't know if I want to go through all of that crap."

"No my friend, it's not like that today. Even the government hacks have moved into the computer world. Here's what a buddy of mine told me about how the deal is done these days." Frank said to Tony.

"Okay, let's hear it." Tony prompted Frank as the two of them lifted their glasses; Frank's a draft beer and Tony's his favorite, the Rob Roy.

Frank began by thanking Tony for the drink, and then went into the details of applying for and collecting unemployment benefits. The steps enumerated by Frank were as follows:

Show up at the local Unemployment Insurance Office. In Illinois its called the Department of Employment Security.

Sit down at a computer and input the required information, name, SS Number, type of work you are seeking, former employer, etc.

Talk to a councilor.

Go home and wait for a debit to your bank account.

Once each week log in via the computer.

Indicate that you continue to be unemployed.

State where it was that you sought employment. (This step may require the use of your imagination.)

This can go on for nearly two years, so what's the hurry to find a job?

Upon the completion of his statement Frank inquired, "Any questions?"

Tony shot back, "C'mon Frank, it can't be that easy. If it was tons of people would be doing it."

"Guess what my friend, millions of people are doing it. For a lot of them they are doing better being unemployed than they did while working. I could give you a nuts and bolts example of that, but let's just assume what I have told you is the truth. Okay?" Frank said as he signaled the bartender that a refill was in order.

"Alright. I think I will go down tomorrow and check it out. If you're right I'll buy another round. If not, you owe me, deal?

"Deal", Frank responded as he lifted his glass to seal the agreement.

u

Aaron Sheffield welcomed agents Adams and Madison to his office. After offering the two IRS employees coffee, attorney Sheffield presented them with an Internal Revenue Service Form 2828, Power Of Attorney. With that form Mr. Sheffield was able to act fully on behalf of his client, Ross Wells.

"I'm somewhat surprised to see the two of you so soon after we met to deal with my client Ross Wells' corporation tax returns. Hopefully we will find a way to deal with the issue at hand in the same manner with which we resolved the corporate tax matter. So let's get at it. What's the reason for a look at my client's return for the Year 2009?" Sheffield inquired.

John Adams opened a file folder that lay before him on the conference table at which the three parties to the meeting had seated themselves. "This is a transcript of the tax return your client and his spouse filed for the Year 2009. We have reason to believe that the income reported on that return was substantially understated."

"I see", lawyer Shefield began. "And what makes you think my client has short-changed Uncle Sam? I might think that the Chicago Cubs will win a

World Series in my life-time too, but that doesn't mean it will actually happen."

"Can you be more specific as to why you have decided to examine the tax return in question? My fees to my clients are based upon the time spent representing them, so a speedy resolution to this matter will be to my client's advantage. A quick wrap up will also free up the two of you, and that will permit you to spend your time in more productive ways."

"Your interest in saving your client some money, and your interest in making me and my partner more productive is certainly appreciated. We also have no interest in wasting time." Adams fired back.

"We have obtained copies of Mr. Wells bank statements, including ATM activity for the Year 2009."

"We also have copies of his Forms W-2 for the year in question. You may recall that an employee of Mr. Wells' company had a tax problem due to a Form W-2 error which originated in the office of Mr. Wells' business. For that reason we have been quite diligent in making certain that we have all of the relevant documents."

"Finally, we have witnesses who are willing to testify to the fact that your client made frequent payments to a line of credit at a local casino."

"Having a line of credit with a casino and gambling with that line is perfectly legal, and the Internal Revenue Service has no problem with that, unless one fails to report winnings when filing a tax returns. From what we have been able to determine so far, we do not think the Wells' return understated gambling winnings."

"Other income is an entirely different matter, and that is why we are here today."

Sheffield reacted. "I'm afraid you have left me in the dark. I'm still not sure of why you are here this morning."

Jim Madison reacted. "Councilor, let's quit the cat and mouse game. Let me lay this out in as simple a manner as possible:"

"Taxpayer A deposits $$ dollars to his casino line of credit."

"Taxpayer A's Forms W-2 for the year equal $ dollars."

"A review of taxpayer's bank statements reveals the fact that disbursements from that account total an amount quite close to the net income shown on the Forms W-2."

"Given the above, we have $$ in deposits with only $ in available money. We are here to find the source of the extra $."

"We've been down this road with you before, so we are asking the same question as we did then. Does that surprise you?"

After a brief pause, Aaron Sheffield told the agents that he new nothing that might point to an answer to their question. He went on to say that he would discuss the matter with his client, and that he would do so with no delay. Finally, the attorney indicated that he would contact them to arrange another meeting in the very near term.

The two agents departed from their meeting with Aaron Sheffield, each with a different feeling about what had taken place that morning.

As the two of them connected the seatbelts in the auto provided to them by their employer, the U S Government, Adams spoke up. "What a waste time that was.

We don't know any more now than we did before we blew almost a full morning dancing with Wells' attorney."

Jim Madison had a different interpretation with respect to the what the meeting had given them.

It was his impression that attorney Sheffield was sincere when he said he did not have any information about unreported income on the part of Ross Ellis. That simplifies the task of getting to the bottom of the barrel of the facts being reviewed, he thought to himself as he started the car and began the drive back to the offices of the IRS.

"I'm afraid I have to differ with you on this one" Madison began.

"I think Sheffield was speaking the truth. I don't think he knew about any income that was not reported on the tax return HE SIGNED as the person who prepared the return. If we are correct in looking for ghost income Sheffield is going to be really pissed, and therefore less gung ho to represent Ross. No Jack, I think it was a productive morning."

Adams responded, "You-re the old-timer in this game, so I guess you know what you are doing. But as far as I'm concerned, they're all lying and will say anything to save their skins."

"Of course they are, my friend. What we have going for us is their desire for self-preservation. We need to play one off against the other until the key bit of information is revealed. Don't feel bad if you didn't pick up on Sheffield's body language. It takes time."

"Our next step is to bring in Mr. D'Angelo and inform him of the taxes and penalties he owes due to the failure to report the gambling winnings of Mrs. D'Angelo. That information may make information we need flow a bit more freely. If you recall, when we last met with him he always wanted to check with some other person further up the line before answering our inquiries. Hopefully that pattern won't continue." Madison said.

Upon arriving back at the office, Madison made a telephone call to Tony's former boss, Joey. He made the call, even though they couldn't believe it, because neither could come up with a telephone number for Tony.

With the required number in hand, Madison reached Tony and made arrangements for a meeting in the offices of the IRS.

U

A week after that telephone call Tony sat down for a meeting with Adams and Madison in their offices at 10:00 AM. Jim Madison spoke first: Good morning Tony, how's thing going?"

Tony replied, "Not real well, and as far as I'm concerned, being here cancels out all chances of a good morning. Let's get down to business."

Adams then laid out the details. "We have spoken with your wife concerning your 2009 income tax return. From that conversation we have learned that a substantial amount of income was not included in the first Form 1040 that you filed, nor was it included in the amended return you subsequently filed. Would you care to comment about that fact?"

"Comment?" What the hell am I supposed to say? You talk to my wife, who lies like a rug, and all of a sudden some income pops up from nowhere. What did you promise her to get her to come up with the story you wanted to hear?" Tony ranted.

"I'm afraid it's not that simple Tony. We have outside information that verifies the income information. Your wife is a big-time gambler, Tony. Did you know that?" Adams queried.

"I found out she was gambling, but I don't know what "Big Time" means." Tony answered.

"As far as we are concerned gambling in excess of $50,000 is big time, and one Laura D'Angelo easily qualifies. The bottom line of this whole deal is that substantial taxes may be due, plus penalties and interest. And as we have mentioned numerous times before, you filed a joint return with your spouse, and that makes the two of you both jointly and separately responsible for all money due the government." John Adams offered with no hint of sympathy in his voice.

Tony pled, "How much is due? I'm not working as you found out when you called Joey Labriola."

"We're not sure because we haven't crunched the numbers yet, but with income in the thousands I'm sure the taxes are in the five figures as well." Jim Madison replied.

"Of course we can probably work out a payment plan for you." he continued.

"How generous of you. I'm overwhelmed with your concern for my pocketbook." Tony snapped back.

Madison responded, "Actually we do have some concern for your well-being, and we are not at all interested in seeing you get the shaft in this matter. We also have an ulterior motive for making the following offer."

"There is a provision in the law that allows a person to avoid a tax liability if it can be shown that the taxpayer did not know, or have any reason to know that income was not being included in the tax return he/she signed. Actually a form exists for that purpose and it is Form Number 8857—<u>Request For Innocent Spouse Relief</u>. Additionally, there is another form, Number 12507—<u>Innocent Spouse Statement</u>."

"Jack and I are willing to work with you to complete the 8857, and we will include a statement supporting your position on the Form 12507. We believe that by doing so you will escape the tax liability. But, we need something from you in return."

"Like what?" Tony asked.

Adams picked up the ball, "You've been involved with us long enough, and you're smart enough to know that the basic inquiry goes like this: two plus two should equal four, but if it comes out five, something is missing. What we have here is a lot of gambling, but we don't know for sure what the source of the gambling stakes was. That's where you may come in to help us, and to help yourself, of course."

He went on, "We believe that the money came from Ross Wells, and we think you already knew that. We have bank and payroll records for the year in question, and those things don't support expenditures of the magnitude that we are discussing here. We're hoping you can shed some light on the missing link. What do you say Tony?"

"Yeah, I knew that Wells was giving my wife money, and I know my wife was blowing the money at the Horseshoe Casino. What I don't know is how much money was changing hands. Are you asking me how Wells got his hands on the money?"

"That's exactly what we want to hear from you Tony." Adams prodded Tony.

"And you're going to help me get the extra taxes off of my back, right?" Tony asked.

u

Once again the agents assured Tony that he was correct. One of the agents produced a copy of the Form 8857 and showed it to Tony, and indicated that completing this form was the first step needed to relieve Tony of the burden of extra taxes and penalties.

Tony responded by asking how he might be sure that the agents could be trusted, and was told he would have to just take a chance.

"Okay, I guess I'll go along with the program. Where did Wells get the extra cash? That's the 64 dollar question. Right?" Tony began.

Adams immediately answered, "Yes sir, that's the big question.

"Okay, here's all I know", Tony began. You know that Wells' company is in the business of leasing slot machines to small businesses, mainly neighborhood taverns. The tavern owner gets to keep half of the net losses from each machine. A company person comes around once a week and clears out the machines."

"That person is not me. My job was to just keep tabs on the businesses and deal with any complaints they might have."

"This may be your answer. The machines are rigged so that they record money played at fifty percent of actual. That is, if the machine reads $100 it actually took in $200. I think the company run by Wells records the amount shown on the machine printout and banks that amount of money. I don't know what happens to the other half of the money. Does that help?" Tony concluded.

Madison jumped at the question, "Absolutely, that's exactly what we needed. Thank you Tony."

"Tony came back with, "So now what happens?"

Agent Adams explained to Tony that there was nothing for him to do at the moment. First the agents would need to meet with Wells, and then again with Tony's wife. He expressed an opinion that Tony shouldn't worry about the outcome in the matter.

With that, Tony left the meeting.

"Pardon the corn, my friend, but we just hit the jackpot." Adams stated firmly.

u

Less than two weeks after the meeting between Tony and the two IRS agents Aaron Sheffield's secretary informed him that Mr. Ross Wells was on the line and had asked to speak with him. Sheffield pressed to appropriate button on the phone and began, "Hello Ross, What's on your mind?"

Wells, in a rather agitated state, indicated that he had received a registered letter from the IRS and its content looked very serious. He went on to say that he wanted to meet with Sheffield to determine how he should respond to the letter.

After a brief pause attorney Sheffield stated his position: "I'm afraid I won't be able to do that Ross. You will have to find someone else to represent you, or you can do it yourself."

Again, this time with the sound of desperation in his voice, Ross reacted, "What? What am I supposed to do? Why are you saying no? I've always compensated you well in the past. I don't get it?"

'You may not believe it Ross, but money isn't everything. There are things such as honesty, integrity, trust and morality. In the past I have earned your trust because I lived those virtues in my dealings with you. Unfortunately it seems to have been a one-way street." Ross explained.

"I still don't get it Aaron. What are you talking about?" Ross pressed on.

Sheffield responded, this time more forcibly. "I prepared your income tax returns for you for several years. I signed each of those returns, and doing so put my professional reputation on the line. I recently learned that you lied to me when you provided me with the tax return data, resulting in false returns to which I appended my signature."

He went on, "I can't think of anything more detrimental to a client/professional relationship than lying or making misleading statements on the part of either party to an association. Hence continuing to represent you is out of the question."

"Secondly, in an attempt to repair my professional reputation, I must distance myself from you as quickly as possible."

"But it's all hearsay Aaron. The Feds haven't proved anything yet, so why such a hasty decision?" Ross asked.

u

This time, with anger in his voice, Sheffield responded, "Ross, what you just said is a perfect example of why I can't and won't deal with you any more. You have not admitted or denied the fact that income was not reported on the returns I prepared. Further, assuming the Government is correct, you have not offered an apology for lying to me. Your only interest seems to be in getting off of the hot seat, not in doing what is the right thing to do."

Sheffield concluded the conversation with, "Ross, find a dictionary and look up the word AMORAL. I think you will readily relate to the behavior described in the dictionary's definition. Let me put it into words even you can understand: It's not what's right or wrong, it's about what's good for me."

With that, Aaron ended the telephone call. He then instructed his secretary to not accept any calls from Ross Wells.

u

At about that same time on the same day agents Adams and Madison were meeting with Laura D'Angelo.

Jim Madison began the conversation.

"Mrs. D'Angelo we have reviewed the records of your gambling activity at the Horseshoe Casino, and as we indicated to you before, the gambling winnings constitute taxable income. We also told you that we would do what we might to relieve the income tax burden stemming from that activity, and we have done that."

Agent Adams picked up the conversation. "It turns out that your losses far exceeded your winnings. From an income tax perspective, that's good news because losses are deductible to the extent of your winnings. Hence, you have no tax liability in connection with your gaming activities."

"Oh, that's great news!" Laura offered.

Immediately, Adams came back to the subject at hand. "I'm afraid is isn't quite that simple Mrs. D'Angelo. We still have to deal with the source of the money with which you carried out your gambling activity."

"The money used in your gambling came from a man named Ross Wells, and the funds advanced to you were not in the form of a gift because you provided some services, on a regular basis, in exchange for the money."

Given that all of the above is true, it seems you were, in fact, self-employed, to put it politely. The earnings from self-employment activities are subject to both income and self-employment taxes."

Laura simply sagged down into the chair in which she was seated. She had no idea of what to say, or what excuse she might conger up. The agents remained silent, letting their words sink into Laura's thought processes. The tension in the room was almost palpable.

Finally she spoke up. "I don't know what to say. What can I do?"

Jim Madison responded to Laura's question. "There really isn't very much you can do, I'm afraid. Contrary to what you might be thinking, we really don't enjoy meetings of this nature. Yes, we relish nailing the wise guys who think they can out maneuver Uncle Sam. And we are not having a very good time this morning. But we are sworn to carry out the law, and that is what this is all about.

He went on, "We are paid well by the citizens of our great country to enforce the law. We are not paid to make life miserable for people like you."

"We can help you to file an amended tax return for the year in question. There may be some out-of-pocket expenditures that would qualify as deductions from your self-employment income. Additionally we can assist you in setting up a payment plan. And, of course, there is no possibility that you would be doing any time in a federal prison."

"I see." Laura began. "And what about that scum of the earth Wells? Does he just walk off scot-free?"

Almost at once, both agents began to respond to Laura's question, but then Adams sat back. Madison continued,

"Does he walk? No way! We have turned his case over to our legal division. Not only will he be paying the back taxes, interest and penalties, he actually has a chance of spending some time behind bars."

"Good!" Laura said, followed by, "And what about my husband, where is he in all of this?

"Mr. D'Angelo seems to have had no knowledge of the activities we have been discussing this morning. Therefore, he should have no financial responsibility stemming from those activities." Adams explained.

"But I don't have any money to use to pay the taxes. I have no idea of what I need to do." The crestfallen Laura pled.

Jack Adams spoke up. "Here's my advice. First try to find some professional person who will work with you. All professionals are expected to do some what is called pro-bono work; that is do the work without accepting any fees for their service."

"Next, you have to look for employment. Both of your children are now in the middle of their teens, so they don't need you to be home all day. You are apparently in good health, you are obviously intelligent and make a good appearance. Finding meaningful employment, even in these difficult times, should not be overly difficult for you. The fact that you have some college credits will surely be of help."

After telling Laura she would be contacted about doing the amended tax return, the meeting was ended.

u

Several weeks later Tony met with Adams and Madison for the purpose of completing the Form 8857 to proclaim his innocent spouse status. With that done, Tony left the office with a bounce in his step that had been absent for too long.

He no sooner sat down in his car when his cell phone went off. Hitting the appropriate button, and with the usual, "Tony here", a familiar voice was heard.

"Hi Tony, Joey here. How's things going?"

Tony replied, "Joey, you couldn't have called at a better time. I just had what I believe was my last meting with the Feds. According to them, I'm homer free!" What's on your mind?"

"You may or may not know it, but Ross Wells is in deep, deep shit. And given that fact, I think there is a good chance that we can take over his business. I think it can be a super deal, even if we play it straight with the tax leeches. What do you say Tony, are you up for it?" Joey coaxed.

With great enthusiasm Tony replied, "You can bet the farm on it. Meet me for lunch at the usual time and place. I'm buying, Partner".